LOVE SO DEEP

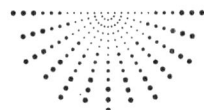

KATHLEEN BALL

Copyright © 2018 by Kathleen Ball

All rights reserved.

No part of this book may be reproduced in any form or by any electronic or mechanical means, including information storage and retrieval systems, without written permission from the author, except for the use of brief quotations in a book review.

❦ Created with Vellum

Love So Deep is dedicated to my readers. Thank you for all of your support. Thank you Jean Joachim for the great title. I want to thank everyone in the Pioneer Hearts Group on Facebook. Thank you Vicki Locey for all your encouragement. Thank you Heather Crispin from Livin' Large Farms for all the love you give to my rescue horse Sparrow. You've taken a frightened starved horse and given her happiness. I dedicate this book to my loves, Bruce, Steven, Colt and Clara because I love them.

CHAPTER ONE

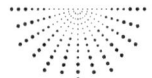

Samantha tried wrapping her scarf around her head, but the weight of the hardened ice kept dragging it down. The naysayers were right, winter came early—very early and with a vengeance. She stared at the pure white snow dotted with Ponderosa pines. Their branches bowed from the snowy burden. She'd doubted her survival the minute they banned her from the wagon train but as she walked away, she grew determined to survive. What a difference a few weeks made. As soon as the storm hit two days ago, her doubts returned.

She took a step and stumbled. The hem of her dress, caked with icy snow, made it hard going. With each step, her feet punched through the snow and sank. Her hands stung from the biting cold. Soon she wouldn't feel them anymore. She knew the signs of frostbite. Pushing herself upright she struggled on, one exhausting step at a time.

The wind howled and she wanted to cry at its sad song. She'd been on her own for two long weeks now. How she hated the pious women she'd traveled with. The death of her parents left her alone and a woman alone was not allowed on the wagon train. The married women believed she'd entice their husbands. The same women whose children she nursed when they were sick. The hypocrisy ate at her soul.

It was either marry Old Thomas or leave. She refused to marry, calling their bluff. Unfortunately, it wasn't a bluff. They threw her a sack of food and a canteen of water and left her behind.

Again, she fell face first into the snow. Struggling to rise, she shook her head. Maybe it'd be easier to just lay there and fall into a forever sleep. Her food was long ago eaten and her strength had held out surprisingly long, but now she wasn't sure it was worth the effort.

A horse nickered and she pushed herself up. Her heart skipped a beat in fright. On the horse sat a huge man covered in animal furs. His rifle lay across his lap.

"Get up," he said, his voice full of anger.

Samantha pushed and struggled until she stood. This was it. She just hoped her death would be painless. Putting her frigid hands on her hips, she brazenly studied him. His slate blue eyes were full of compassion. He held out his hand. She grasped it and he hauled her up in front of him.

"Let's get you warm." He opened his fur coat, pulled her against his warm body, and wrapped them both up. "Where are your people?"

"My people?"

"Yes, do you have a cabin here bouts? You shouldn't be out here alone. It's dangerous and in the snow it's easy to get lost."

Turning her head, she felt his warm breath against her cheek. His full beard brushed against her. "I'm on my own. I was hoping to find a town."

He didn't say anything else as he urged his steed forward. It was slow going in the snow but the horse seemed to know its way. Leaning back against his wide chest, her eyes closed.

She awoke with a start, not recognizing where she was. A fire danced in the massive stone fireplace, but beyond the firelight, it was dark. Pain shot through her hands and feet. It was expected with frostbite but she didn't know just how painful it was until now.

The cabin looked well built out of hand-hewed logs, and no wind came through the walls. It was tiny, but it probably suited the man who rescued her. Sitting up, she waited for her eyes to adjust to the semi-darkness. There was a big pile of furs in one corner, a table with two chairs, and a makeshift kitchen area. Wooden crates hung on the walls to serve as shelves and a roughly put together plank of wood with logs for legs held a few kitchen items and tools.

Above the pile of furs were pegs on which a few items of clothing hung. There was nothing fancy and nothing of convenience but it was warm. She was grateful to have shelter from the cold. The pain in her fingers was the worst and she dreaded looking at them. Slowly she pulled them out from under the covers and to her relief, they weren't blackened with severe frostbite.

The door opened and the man came in, a bundle of firewood in his arms. Kicking the door closed behind him, he then glanced in her direction. "So, you've decided to come back to this world, did ya?"

"How long was I asleep?" Her body tensed, not sure what he had in store for her.

He laid the wood next to the fireplace and threw a log on top of the fire. The flame blazed higher. "Only a day. You sure were hard to thaw, and I'm glad ya was out when I tended your hands and feet. Painful business it is."

"Thank you. They're still hurting. It was nice of you to tend to me. I was afraid I'd lose them. Actually, I figured I was going to die out there. I've never seen snow so early. I wonder how the others fared."

His dark brow rose. "Others? You said you were alone. Damn, I live up here to be away from folks, not to go rescue them." He took off his fur coat and sat down.

"I am, or was, alone. I got kicked off the wagon train and was left to fend for myself." Her voice contained the bitterness she couldn't hide.

"What in tarnation are you talking about? You must have done something pretty awful to be banned from the train."

"Of course."

His blue eyes widened and he ran his hand through his thick black hair. It hung past his shoulders and she wondered when was the last time he'd had it cut. "You might as well tell me. I'm not the type to judge."

"My parents died and they refused to let me travel with them alone. It was either marry old toothless Thomas or be thrown off the train. To my surprise they were serious and when I refused to marry Thomas they filled a sack with a meager amount of food, filled a canteen, and allowed me to take my coat and scarf with me." She paused as all the pain came rushing back. There hadn't even been time to mourn the passing of her dear mother and father.

"Miss, that's—"

"It's Samantha. Samantha Foley."

He nodded. "I'm Patrick McCrery. I have to say that's quite the yarn you're spinning."

She glanced away from his intense eyes. "I wish it was just a story."

"Well now, are ya sure ya weren't inviting the married men to look your way?"

A loud sigh was her reply. She'd thought the people on the wagon train were crazy, but now a stranger believed her capable of luring men. What was it about her that people assumed such an awful thing? "I thought you said no judgment."

"Aye, I did. How long ago did they put you out?"

"I'd say two weeks or so. I tried to follow by foot but they actually threw rocks at me to keep me away. As far as I'm concerned, they left me to die." A tear rolled down her face. "Ouch!" She tried to wipe it away.

"Don't cry. I hate crying. If ya want me to believe your story I will."

Her eyes narrowed. "Just what is it about me that screams whore to you?"

"You have pretty blonde hair, and a man could get lost in those big blue eyes of yours. I have to say you're nicely rounded in the right places. You don't seem very meek either."

"You think I should have married Thomas? He is shiftless and wanted me to be his worker, not a wife. It would have caused trouble since I had no inclination to lay with him. He surely would have beaten me for it too. So, maybe my predicament is my fault. I suppose I chose death over a life of sheer hell."

His face softened a bit but she could see the clouds of doubt in his eyes. "I bet you're hungry. I'll throw something together." There was an edge to his voice and it didn't invite any more conversation.

Lying back down, she figured she might as well try to regain her strength before she was put out again.

PATRICK SQUATTED BEFORE THE FIRE, adding wild onion to his venison stew. It was his winter staple. He wasn't sure what to think. Her story, though far-fetched could be true. He'd heard of worse. Sometimes people on a wagon train turned on each other. Usually they just broke into smaller groups. Who in their right mind would leave a woman behind? There was no way she was as innocent as she claimed.

Glancing over his shoulder, his eyes drank their fill of her. She was beautiful and while sleeping he could imagine her to be an angel, but he knew better. Most people weren't what they showed the world. No, many harbored secrets and prejudices. Samantha, he'd never known a woman with that name before. She was probably supposed to be a boy named Sam and her parents had chosen a female name.

Her honey blonde hair fanned out on the pillow. It'd been a long time since he'd seen a woman so fair. He went to town twice a year for supplies, other than that he lived a mostly solitary life. There were a few neighbors like him, who didn't like the closed-in feel of a town. He tried the town life for a bit but people were not a charitable lot. They never forgave his parents for their supposed sins.

Traps needed checking and he couldn't take the time to indulge himself in his musings. Grabbing his heavy coat, he glanced back at Samantha and went out into the cold. The frigid bite hit him full force and ducking his head against the wind, he made his way to the makeshift barn. His horse, Ahearn, was always ready and willing to go no matter what the weather. He more than earned his name, which meant Lord of Horses in Gaelic.

Leaving a woman to starve and freeze—what was the world coming to? He mounted his horse and off they went to make their way among the traps. He already had a good amount of the finest furs and it made him proud. Hard work always paid off.

They traveled from trap to trap and found nothing. Perhaps the woman brought some bad luck with her. His mother would have prayed over her and sent her on her way. He smiled. He missed his mother but at least he had many fond memories to get him through the hard times. The clouds were rolling into the mountains and they were in for more nasty weather. He turned Ahern toward home and off they went.

A set of small footprints caught his eye. He pulled up on the reins, stopping Ahern and jumped off. The prints looked to be a child's. Did Samantha leave a child behind? She didn't wear a ring. Was she married? He followed them for a while but they disappeared in the blowing snow. Still he searched but he came up empty. It was too damn cold for a child to survive out here but there was nothing else he could do.

Grabbing Ahearn's mane, he jumped onto his back and headed to the cabin. The wind picked up and the sky turned dark. He'd better hurry if he planned to make it home before the next storm blew in.

After getting Ahearn into the barn and dried off, he gave him extra hay and made sure there was water. Grabbing a rope, he fully intended to tie a line from the barn to the house in case there was a white out. More than one person had frozen to death just steps from their houses. A rustling sound in the hayloft caught his attention and he slowly made his way to the pile. A small black shoe stuck out but the rest hid beneath the hay.

"Achoo."

"Come on out, I know you're in there." His words were met with silence.

There was another sneeze and Patrick reached down and brushed the hay off a small child. A boy, a blond-haired, blue-eyed, boy.

"You'll freeze out here and die. Come to the house, your Ma's in there."

The boy's eyes widened but he remained silent. He stretched out both arms to Patrick and he grabbed him up into his arms. The poor child was skin and bone. What type of mother leaves her child out in the snow to die? Samantha had a lot of explaining to do.

"Let's get ya warm and dry. I even have food warming over the fire."

The boy nodded, put his head on Patrick's shoulder, and closed his eyes.

Samantha grabbed a tin plate and ladled some of the venison stew on it. Her stomach growled and her mouth watered. Her clothes were still damp so she grabbed one of Patrick's shirts and put it on. It was huge on her. She rolled up the sleeves and laughed. It practically hung to her feet.

He didn't seem to be one to smile often, but he hadn't tried to have his way with her either. Hoping for a peek outside, she opened the door, but the intense wind immediately pushed her back. It was a struggle to close the door. Hopefully Patrick wasn't too far away.

Her hands and feet still hurt, but not as much as the first time she woke. It was a good sign. Patrick must get supplies somewhere. The nearest town couldn't be too far away. As soon as the storm stopped, she'd be on her way. She hadn't quite figured out what she'd do once she got to town but she was sure there must be a kindly pastor and his wife to take her in for a bit.

Sitting at the table, she ate until she was full. It seemed to be forever since she'd had enough to eat. Supplies on the wagon train had been rationed and the hope for hunting quickly dimmed as the hunters returned day after day with no food.

She took her last bite when the door blew open with a bang. Patrick stood in the doorway, carrying a child and glaring at her. "I found your child. I've heard about bad mothers but dang it ya are as cold hearted as they come. Why no mention of your son? You left him out there to die!"

Quickly standing, she backed up. "That is not my boy. I've never been married."

"Aha! So, the real skinny is coming to light. What happened the rest of the pious folks on the wagon train found out you have a bastard and threw ya out? Did you figure you'd be better off without proof of your sins?"

The back of her legs hit the bed and she immediately sat. "I don't know what you're talking about. That child needs tending. Bring him here."

"What's his name?" he asked as he laid him on the bed.

"How would I know?" She was glad her irritation showed in her voice. The mountain man was pure loco.

"You plan to play out your lies? Your heart must be iced over."

"He is not my child." She began to undress the boy and gasped. His bones were visible and he had more than a few bruises on him.

Patrick gaffed. "I wouldn't want to admit to the treatment of the boy either."

It was getting nearly impossible to keep her temper reined in. "Could you get me some warm water and a bit of muslin if you have it. I'd like to wash him off a bit."

He didn't say a word, he just did as she asked. He watched as she tenderly wiped the dirt away from the boy.

"From his thinness I'd say he'd been on his own for more than a few weeks. How old do you think he is?"

"He's puny enough to pass for three but I reckon he's at least four or so. He was smart enough to hide in my hay."

Samantha nodded. It didn't matter what Patrick thought, she needed to tend to the boy. Someone out there was missing a child and they were probably heartbroken or dead. These mountains were unforgiving. She briefly wondered how the people on the wagon train were faring but dismissed them fast enough. They probably weren't wondering about her.

As soon as she washed the boy up, she tucked him into the massive bed. His eyes opened and he smiled. "Mommy?"

Before she could utter a word, Patrick sat on the edge of the bed. "You're fine now, lad. Your ma is right here. No more worries."

The boy nodded and instantly fell back to sleep.

Patrick stood and crossed his arms in front of him. His expression was thunderous. "Lies upon lies. If the wind wasn't howling like a banshee, I'd put you out. Children are innocents and no matter how they came into the world they deserve the same love as any other child."

She took a deep breath and slowly let it out. What was there to say? He didn't believe one word she said. Why the child called her mommy was a mystery but they did have the same coloring. His ma was probably blonde too. She'd lived a good, honest and respectable life. She obeyed her parents and tried to do what was right. Maybe it was all for naught. Patrick didn't care, he already judged her immoral.

"I hope his parents are alive somewhere and we can reunite them."

He laughed mockingly and shook his head. "Still insisting he's not yours huh? He did call you mommy. I think it's proof enough. You can stop with your untruths now."

She gave him a sad smile, walked by him, and grabbed one of the chairs. She put it closer to the fireplace and sat down. Maybe the storm would be over soon.

She had nerve, sticking to her story. How could she accept shelter from him when her child was out in the blizzard? Then there were the bruises on the child's body. He had to fight the urge to give her a bruise or two. He'd never hit a woman before and he didn't intend to start now, even if she did deserve it.

The cabin felt smaller, more closed in with her in it. She wasn't going to stay without working for her keep. "Can ya cook?"

She jerked her head and glanced at him. "Yes."

"What about keeping a place clean and the like?"

"I can do it all. Don't worry, I don't intend to sit around waiting for the snow to subside. I appreciate all you have done for me but I'll be lighting out as soon as possible."

"And the boy?"

"I don't even know his name. I know you don't believe me, but it's true. No, the boy will not be coming with me."

He grunted. "No sense arguing about it now. The snow will be there for months to come."

Her eyes widened and her throat dried. "Months?"

"Yes, months. You're in the high country. Once it snows it's pretty much going to keep snowing until spring." He briefly enjoyed her horrified expression, until he realized he was stuck with her. "You mentioned your parents died."

"My mother started to grow weaker and weaker and no matter what we tried, she died. It was only three weeks into the drive. My dad fell off his horse and broke his neck about two weeks ago. It was his turn to hunt and I drove the wagon. His horse showed up, dragging him." She closed her eyes. "It wasn't pleasant to see. We buried him and they banned me in the same day. I'll never get over losing my parents but being turned away hurt. I nursed many of the people on the train, especially the children. I helped to birth two, but in the end it didn't matter."

Her sadness tugged at his heart. "They banned the two of ya?"

"Two? Oh, you still think he's mine. No, they left me alone." She bristled.

"I see." He didn't see at all.

"Do you like living here alone? How far are you from town?"

"I enjoy my solitude. The town is a good two to three days away. I don't go in very often."

"Sounds lonely." Her voice grew soft.

"It can be but it's better than the alternative."

"The alternative?"

He started to reply but a cry from his bed drew his attention. They both went over to see the boy. He sat next to him and was surprised when he wrapped his arms around him and called him pa. Bewildered he turned and locked gazes with Samantha. She just shrugged.

"Do you know what your name is?"

"Yes, Sir, I'm Brian." He nodded hesitantly.

"I'm Patrick and, well, you know your ma."

Brian just nodded, his eyes widened as he stared at his mother. Then he smiled.

"How'd you end up outside all alone?" Patrick asked gently.

"I dunno. I don't think I know. How?" He raised his eyebrows waiting for an answer.

"Perhaps your ma knows."

"I don't think so. I don't think anyone knows."

"What's the last thing you remember?"

"I was sleeping in the back of a wagon. A man was takin' me to live with him. He said I'd be able to do a lot of work."

Patrick gave her a pointed look. "Doesn't sound like a good situation."

Brian smiled. "Here is better. Got any food?"

"I bet your ma could get you some food. I'd like some too."

Samantha stiffened but didn't say a word. She went to the pot hanging above the fire and stirred the stew before she ladled it onto two plates. She grabbed the two other forks he owned and brought them both food. "It's hot."

"Thank you."

She stared at him for a moment and then nodded. "You're welcome."

He sat on the edge of the bed and out of the corner of his eye, he saw Brian watching him and taking a bite when he did. He wanted to chuckle but thought it best not to. He wasn't sure what was going on but they'd be stuck with each other for a while and they needed to work things out. The first thing he needed to do was find Samantha's dress. The occasional peek at her shapely legs was starting to give him ideas. Ideas he had no business thinking. Maybe she would be interested in a relationship with him but he didn't want any children to come of it. It was better to keep his mind on other things.

"I'll go hunting tomorrow and see what I can find. For some reason my traps were all empty today. I don't rightly remember that ever happening before."

Brian hung his head. "Solomon stoled them."

His brow furrowed. "Solomon?"

"Yep, he's the man I belong to. He took all your animals and reset the traps. I must have fallen off the wagon."

"He has a wagon up here? It's sure to get stuck."

"We ain't from around here. We've been traveling and Solomon saw Ma get throwed away so he followed her but he said she was a tricky one and hard to find. He always took the animals. He likes the fur. Soon we were going to hunt for gold."

"Brian, I want ya to think hard before you answer my next question. Is she really your ma?"

Brian's hands shook but he looked Patrick straight in the eye. "Yes sir, she's my ma."

CHAPTER TWO

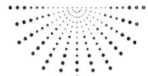

*T*oo stunned to protest, she stood there and didn't say a thing. Why in the world would this child claim to be hers? Things were bad enough around here as far as trust went. There was intelligence in Brian's eyes, and she had a feeling he knew exactly what he was saying.

"Well if you two are done eating, I'll just get to washing the dishes."

Patrick stood and he seemed taller than she remembered. "I'd like to talk to ya, outside."

"I'd be happy to as soon as my dress is dry."

He looked her up and down then nodded. "I bet it'll be dry soon."

Swallowing hard, she nodded. "Yes, soon."

She poured warm water into a basin and washed the few dishes and finally the pot—taking her time, trying to delay their talk. What was there to say? He didn't believe her. Her word had always been good enough while her parents were alive, then suddenly she wasn't to be trusted. None of it made sense to her at all. Hadn't she been through enough? Sighing, she dried her hands and grabbed her dress. She was lucky to be alive.

"Where shall I change?"

He blinked at her and looked around. "I guess we'll just turn our backs."

"Fine." She waited until they had their backs to her and quickly changed into her dress. "I'll need my coat."

"That piece of cloth won't keep you warm. Come on, we can share mine."

Her face grew hot. "I don't think that would be proper."

"Out here we work with what we've got. Come on." He put the giant fur coat on and held his arm out for her to get under. "See, not so bad."

It was much too close but she didn't utter a word as they walked outside in accord. He took her to the barn, which was almost as cold as the outdoors, but it kept the wind off them.

"What's your horse's name?"

"Ahearn, it means Lord of Horses in Gaelic."

"I see."

"Samantha, ya must know my confusion and my exasperation. There are too many things that don't add up and I'm sorry but ya come out at the losing end. I don't know ya, but the child inside says you're his ma and I believe him. I don't know what led to ya both being out in the forest but ya didn't even mention him once while I was rescuing you. What do you have to say for yourself?"

She tensed and her chin began to wobble. It was all too much. Her whole life had turned on end and now this. "All I know is the truth. He is not my son. I have never lain with a man. I have never tried to steal any woman's husband and I have never tried to entice a man, ever. I am from a good, God-fearing family and I don't understand any of this. If you want to put me out, do it now before I begin to like you or something."

"There's not much to like. I'll not be putting ya out but I'll not be trusting ya either. I expect ya to treat your son with care. Those bruises came from somewhere. Perhaps not from you. My best guess is they came from your man, Solomon."

"I don't know why I even bother talking to you." Quick as lightning she unwrapped herself from his coat and ran out into the blizzard. The light from the lamp led her back to the cabin stairs and by the time she got inside, she felt chilled to the bone. She drew a blanket around her but she couldn't get her teeth to stop chattering.

The door slammed open. Patrick looked at her and began to mutter something about how people don't use the brains God gave them. "Let me get you some tea."

"You have tea up here?"

"I'm not much of a coffee drinker. Brian, move over so I can put your ma next to you."

Before she could object, he lifted her and tucked her into the bed next to her supposed son. As soon as she had Brian alone, he had a lot to answer for.

The gentleness of Patrick surprised her as he prepared her tea, plumped up her pillow and made sure she was warming up. He handed her the tin cup and told her to be careful, it was hot. He was a strange, contrary man, to say the least. If it truly ended up a long, hard winter as Patrick predicted, she'd have to find a way to get along with him. It meant she was going to have to swallow her pride. She had a feeling it would involve a lot of tongue biting.

As she sipped her tea, she pondered her quandary. How had everything gotten so turned around? It hadn't been too long ago she was helping her parents pack the wagon for a new start in Oregon. Her father already purchased land and made a deal with a rancher for some cattle. It was an exciting time. Then her mother died and she'd thought she couldn't go on, only to have her father die. She assumed she could drive the team herself and continue.

They all turned on her and no matter how hard she thought about it, no answers came. It started with Stinky Sullivan and Old Thomas and ended up with her elderly friend Eunice throwing the bag of food at her feet. They took her wagon and left her there. She sat up straighter and her jaw dropped.

Patrick glanced at her. "What?" His impatience laced his voice.

"They stole my wagon and the money."

Patrick stood up and walked to her side, taking the cup out of her hands. "What money?"

Running her hands over her face, she tried to take a deep calming breath. "No wonder Stinky was so insistent I leave with nothing. He started the rumors about me the second my father died. I hardly had him buried before others began to snub me. The deed to my papa's land was in the wagon." Her hands clenched and unclenched the fur covers. "Stinky even told me to be sure no papers were on my papa before we buried him. I'm so stupid."

"Stinky?" Brian giggled.

Her head ached. "Yes, Stinky Sullivan. He and my pa were making plans to ranch together. He had his eye on me but they don't call him Stinky for nothing."

Brian laughed louder. "I wouldn't want that name."

"He's a polecat!"

This time Patrick joined Brian in laughing. The urge to cry left her. There was nothing she could do about it now. "At least I know why. My hurt by their actions grew daily, and I couldn't figure out what I had done wrong. Dang, I even cared for their children when they were sick. We spent a lot of time together, and I grew to think of them as family." A deep sigh escaped her and she lay back until her head hit the pillow. It hadn't been her fault after all. They had her almost convinced she was a bad person. Peacefulness filled her soul and she stared up at the log ceiling, hoping her parents were together in heaven watching over her.

"Are ya alright, lass?" His dark eyes filled with compassion and one dark brow rose.

"Yes. Lass? Might you have a wee bit of Irish in ya?" she asked in her best Irish brogue.

"My pa was born there, County Tyrone. He loved America but often longed to be back home."

"My papa had lots of stories from when he was a boy there in County Mayo. He always had the same longing. He left a lot of family back there."

When he smiled, he looked much younger. His grin was almost boyish and his eyes had a bit of sparkle in them. What a transformation from the brooding look he usually had. It was a very nice change indeed.

BOTH OF HIS guests were sleeping and he couldn't help but watch them. What to make of the whole situation, he had no idea. Samantha, so positive of her story and Brian very convincing about his. The boy had the same coloring as Samantha. Blood would always tell. It was a saying he'd heard repeatedly. It was the very reason he lived away from the rest of the world. He'd lived in so-called polite society most of his life but as soon as his pa died, he took off. There wasn't anything or anyone in town for him. People put up with his pa well enough, but their good will didn't extend to his half-breed son.

No sense bemoaning his past. He, like Brian, was just an innocent lad. No one would lay another hand on the boy. No one helped him, but he'd do the right thing and help someone who couldn't defend himself.

Grabbing his bedroll from the corner, behind his pile of furs, he spread it out in front of the fireplace and lay on it. Sleep came easier than anticipated.

The sounds of whispers woke him with a start and quick as lightning he was on his feet. His face heated at the startled expressions on Samantha and Brian's faces. "Sorry, I forgot ya were here. It's good to be fast on your feet out here."

Samantha nodded but Brian's brows furrowed. Poor child probably had to be fast on his feet to try to avoid beatings. Though it didn't appear he'd been successful. His eyes narrowed and he shook his head. How could his ma allow it to happen? Many women were afraid of their husbands and were beaten too, but Samantha wasn't full of marks on her body.

She hadn't asked about him undressing her when he rescued her and put her to bed. It was just as well. It would have made for some awkward conversation. It was an image he couldn't forget. She was beautiful, the type of woman who would never allow him to touch her.

"Good morning! If you'll move your things from the fireplace I'll make us some tea and breakfast."

He closed his eyes—a morning person he wasn't, but apparently Samantha was extra cheery in the morning. After he folded up his bedroll and put it back in the corner, he pulled on his boots and grabbed his coat. "I need to... I'm going to get more wood and water."

"You're leaving?" Brian's eyes widened and he wrapped his arms around Patrick's middle.

Patrick's heart tugged. "I'll be back, don't worry." The boy still had doubt written all over his face. "Really, I'll be as quick as I can."

Brian nodded and Samantha leaned down, putting her arms around his small frame. "You can help me cook."

He nodded again but he didn't take his gaze off Patrick.

"Go on." She moved her hand as if waving him out the door.

Once outside, he paused and looked back at the cabin. So much for solitude. It was a shame the poor boy didn't trust anyone. It was one of those life lessons learned the hard way. He hoped Solomon was out there frozen to death. No, death was too easy; he hoped the bastard was suffering in the blizzard without food or shelter. He made his way to the barn and Ahearn snorted in greeting.

"Guess we're going to have a few extra mouths to feed for a bit. Samantha is too bright and happy. I mean she brightens the place up, but I'm used to gloomy silence. And the boy, if someone doesn't teach him to trust soon, he may never trust anyone."

Ahern butted his shoulder with his nose. "I know, old boy, just like me. Looks like it's going to be snowshoes for a while. The snow is getting too deep for me to take ya with me. Wish I was alone. I'd hunt down that thieving Solomon and get my furs back, but I promised I'd stay. Glad I have ya to talk to." He patted Ahern's muscled flank and walked toward the cabin. He'd stick around for the day but starting tomorrow, he had traps to check.

"Why do you keep insisting I'm your ma? You know it's not true." She tried to keep her voice gentle but she wasn't feeling so nice now. She'd been at it for at least a quarter hour but Brian wouldn't budge.

Crossing her arms in front of her, she tapped her foot. "You're afraid of this Solomon guy, I get it. It's understandable, but you can't go around calling me your ma. I've never been married for Pete's sake. Patrick didn't think too highly of me before you came along and now he thinks I'm an awful mother on top of it all. I don't know what to do or say."

Brian refused to look at her. He kept his gaze on the floor, barely blinking as though he didn't hear her.

"Brian? Answer me please."

The door opened and Patrick came in with a rush of cold air. "He has no respect for you. He'd answer ya if he did. Can't say I blame him." He set a pail of water on the floor then walked to the fireplace and dropped the wood beside it. He took off his winter gear and his brow arched when he finally noticed her glare.

"I'm only telling you the truth of things."

"You wouldn't know the truth if it was right in front of you. How far is it to town, did you say?" She couldn't stay anywhere near Patrick and his judgmental gazes anymore.

"A couple days by horse, maybe a week walking."

She huffed and put breakfast on the table. "You have laid in a lot of supplies."

"Living up here, I get snowed in." He sat down and Brian quickly followed suit.

She waited for Patrick to offer her the chair but the offer never came. So much for him being any type of gentleman. "We seem to be one chair short."

"Never had a need for more than two." He helped himself to a biscuit, bit into it and smiled. "You're a fair cook."

Ignoring him, she filled a plate and sat on the bed. She had to admit it was the best food she'd had in a good while. Her ability to cook over a fire came in handy. "Do you think there is any way I can catch up to the wagon train? I'd like to get back what's mine."

He cocked his head and gave her a sad smile. "No, lass. Either they are still traveling or if caught in the snow, they could be anywhere. There's no guarantee they'll survive. Your group must have gotten a late start and with the early winter they may not make it."

His words saddened her. She'd made good friends who'd turned against her, but she would never wish them harm. The wind howled loudly. "We left early enough. The group was full of complainers, and we didn't get very far before someone insisted we stop and rest. My parents were concerned but the wagon master, Chigger Graham, didn't seem to care."

"Chigger? That's a whole different story. He's been known to rob people and ride off. Bet he's sitting in a nice warm cabin somewhere in these mountains right now. The murdering

bast—"

"Language."

"What?"

"There is an impressionable child here and you need to watch your language."

His jaw dropped, tempting her to laugh.

"It's not the first time he's done something like this. Did most of the folks already have property bought?"

A chill went through her. "Yes, why?"

"Aw hel..heck. There is no property. He took your money and handed out phony deeds."

A lump formed in her throat. "He had a map. We picked our property. It was all official."

"I'm sorry, lass. It's a hard blow and I bet that feller Stinky was in on it too."

Tears formed in her eyes and she turned her head away. She'd hoped to find her property and confront Stinky Sullivan. They'd been taken for everything they had, including lives. If only her papa hadn't been so keen on going out West. The tears began to flow down her face. How? Why?

Brian took the plate from her hands and set it on the bed. He climbed onto her lap and hugged her. Don't cry, Ma. I hate it when you cry."

PATRICK SWUNG the axe into the air and brought it down with great force. The wood he split went flying in opposite directions. He couldn't stomach her lies any longer. Watching her hold Brian on her lap as she cried cinched it. Why did she keep denying the boy? She was a bit touched in the head. She'd better not lay a hand on the lad or she'd have to answer to him.

He gathered the wood he'd chopped, dropped a bit of it on the huge woodpile he had, and brought the rest inside the cabin. Usually chopping wood was a cure for any restlessness he felt, but it didn't help this time. It was more than restlessness, sure, he needed to see to his traps, but it wasn't a driving urge. It was the woman. Something about her disturbed him and it wasn't her lying ways. He'd learned long ago not to touch a white woman but she tempted him.

And her not knowing she was a temptation was the worst part. She didn't view him in that manner. He was just someone who happened upon her in the frozen mountains. After spending most of the morning in the cold, he was ready to warm up. Damn, he'd never hesitated to go into his house before.

With his arms loaded with firewood, he used his elbow to lift the latch on the door. He stepped into the cabin and was hit smack in the face with wet undergarments hanging from a rope strung from one wall to the opposite wall. "What the…"

"Oops, sorry. Darn, I hope you didn't get them dirty. It's not easy to wash clothes in here."

He ducked, walked under the line, and was awe struck. She wore his shirt again but somehow she looked almost enticing in it. "Helped yourself to my clothes again?"

She smiled and her eyes lit up. "Washed all the clothes I had and you know it isn't much. Washed Brian's and I washed your smalls."

"You washed my under things?"

"I figured I may as well since I had the water good and hot."

He glanced at Brian, who was sitting on the bed with a fur wrapped around his scrawny body. Their gazes locked and Brian's red face and the look of annoyance almost made his lips twitch. Instead, he gave him a nod of understanding.

"Wish I had more extra clothes."

"I have it figured out if you'll help me."

His eyes furrowed and he studied her. "What do ya have going on in that sweet head of yours?"

She blushed. "I just thought we could make clothes out of buckskin. You seem to have plenty."

"I don't know the first thing about making clothes. I get mine in trade. Besides, I don't have anything for you to sew with. I broke my last needle stitching up a gash on my head."

She grabbed Brian's clothes off the line. "I could use your knife to cut out the pattern and with pieces of leather strips I think I could hold the buckskin together to form clothes. I'd like to take a closer look at yours to see how they are put together." Walking to the bed, she handed Brian his dry clothes. "Here, now you have clean clothes."

Brian stared at the clothes. "Thanks, Ma. It's been a mighty long time since I had clean clothes."

She sighed, gave Patrick a sidelong glance, and cringed. He hoped she saw his disapproval. What child was ever happy about clean clothes? None of it made any sense and it was a dilemma.

"You might as well take off your clothes so I can wash them."

Shaking his head, he sat down. "I don't think it's a good idea."

"You don't want clean clothes?" She crossed her arms before her and frowned.

"Ya see, ya have the only other shirt on."

"Oh. You can sit on the bed wrapped in furs."

He narrowed his eyes at her. "I'm not going to spend my day sitting on the bed like some young whelp."

Shrugging her shoulders, she looked away. "Fine. I just figured a grown man would own more than one pair of pants."

"I did until I cut my leg a few weeks back. There was so much blood, I burned the pants."

"You're hurt? Why didn't you say so? How bad is it? I'd better take a look at it to make sure it's healing properly."

She came toward him and he put his hand up. "I don't like to be fussed over."

She still came to him. "I'm not fussing. In case you haven't realized it, you are the only thing keeping us warm and fed. I wouldn't want anything to happen to you."

"Ya washed your hair. It's pretty."

She gave him a pointed look. "Don't try changing the subject. I intend to see your wound. I can be very stubborn you know."

"So I noticed," he mumbled.

"I don't know what you said but I'm sure it wasn't polite. Now I insist on seeing it. Did it need stitches?"

"No, I cauterized it with my knife. I'm sure it's fine." The cabin suddenly became too crowded. "I'm fine."

Samantha eyed him with suspicion. "I'll give you some time to get used to the idea, but I will see to that leg." She turned and walked to the clothesline, rearranging the garments. He could tell by the tautness of her spine she was mad. It was too bad. He didn't want her touching him anywhere.

In his clean clothes, Brian approached him. Putting his elbows on Patrick's knees he looked up at him. "Don't make Ma mad. You'd better show her the cut." He nodded his head solemnly.

He would have laughed at the seriousness but Brian had been on the other side of mad. "Maybe I'll show her later. I wouldn't want to be the cause of upset."

"No, sir, you don't."

"Been getting enough to eat here?"

Brian stood up straight and pulled his shoulders back. "I sure have. Best food I've had in a very long time. Solomon, he only let me eat what he didn't. Some nights he'd eat big and there wasn't much for me. You have to be grateful for what you got."

"Does your ma do the cooking at home?"

"Ain't got no—" His eyes grew wide and he slapped his hands over his mouth. Slowly he took his hands from his face and smiled. "I mean yes, she's a good cook." Brian smiled and shrugged.

Something stunk and maybe, just maybe, it was Brian who was the stinking liar. Before he opened his mouth, Samantha stood behind Brian with her hands on his shoulders. "It's fine Brian. It's no use trying to lie." She gave his shoulder a squeeze and stared. "You see, you were right all along. Brian is mine. I don't know why I denied it. I mean, I really have no idea."

"Lass, ya are full of malarkey. But I do admire the way ya stuck up for the boy."

As her shoulders relaxed, she let out a big sigh. "I can explain."

"I think I know the way of it. Brian, I don't cotton to no

lyin', but ya did it to keep yourself safe. It could be considered by some as a smart move. Just like Samantha claiming ya just now, she did it to protect ya. I'm not throwing either one of ya out, so the truth from now on out would be appreciated."

Brian got up and flung himself at him. "I didn't want to lie."

"It's okay. We'll get it all worked out."

Glancing at Samantha, his insides warmed at the big smile of approval she sent his way. His stomach did a flip and he told himself to look away but he just couldn't. Basking in her smile was a feeling like no other. She made him feel worthy.

Finally, he blinked and looked away. "So, the wagon train story is true." He pulled Brian up onto his knee. "Let's hear the real Solomon story."

Brian's eyes widened and he shook his head.

"It's fine. I just need to know if someone will be looking for ya. Is he your pa?"

"No…no, sir. He found me in a place called Denver. My parents had died and the orphanage was a damned place. I slipped out one night intending to make it on my own."

"How old are you really?"

"I'm seven."

Patrick nodded. "Go on."

"I was making my way down an alley, trying to figure my next move when Solomon caught me. He's really tall and he's plenty strong. Not as big as you, but big. He lifted me like a sack of potatoes, hauled me to his wagon, and knocked me out. I woked up and it was mornin' and my hands and feet were tied. I thought for sure he was gonna kill me. He kept traveling west that day, barely looking at me, and I didn't get no food or water. I remember I was a might thirsty. A few days later he untied my hands and let me eat his scraps and he gave me a mouthful of water. He tied my hands again and that's how we went for a long time."

"Did he say why he was heading west?" Patrick asked.

"He talked about gold and silver and treasure along the way. Oper…oper…opportunities were plentiful."

Samantha walked to them and stroked Brian's shoulder. "I'm sorry he stole you. You're safe now."

Patrick watched her hand on Brian's shoulder, comforting him in a motherly way. He couldn't remember if his mother had ever done the same for him. She'd died when he was young and his father wasn't an affectionate man. Hell, he wasn't even nice half the time. He was glad he didn't have the same hunger for whiskey as his father.

He stood Brian up and then stood himself. He grabbed his coat, rifle, and snowshoes. "I'm going to check a few of the closer traps." He opened the door then turned toward Samantha. "Your idea about the buckskin is a good one." Out into the cold he went.

CHAPTER THREE

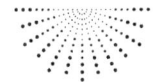

"I can't believe you're seven. I should have figured it all out. Really there is a big difference between four and seven," Samantha commented as she cut Brian's hair. "Stop squirming, these shears aren't the sharpest."

"My hair was just fine before you started hacking at it."

"Don't you want to look good?"

Laughter filled the kitchen. "For what? Have you looked at Patrick? His hair is much longer and he has a beard. There ain't no one to see us."

"Isn't not ain't and we see each other."

"So?" Brian turned to look at her.

"I don't know, honestly. A person should always strive to look and act civilized."

"Is that why they kicked you off that wagon train? You were too bossy?"

She put the shears on the table and placed her hands on her hips. "No, that is not the reason and I am anything but bossy."

The door flew open and Patrick crossed over the threshold carrying two big fish with him. "Bossy huh? Ya know you're right." He smiled at her and raised his eyebrows. "How are ya on cooking fish?" His smile lightened her heart.

"'bout fair to middlin'. It'll just have to be a chance you take." The softening of his eyes caused her face to warm. His handsome, strong features intrigued her but nothing could ever come of it. This was not the kind of life she dreamed of. The cabin gave her shelter but she needed a community. What about church or school for Brian? She took the offered fish and when she saw they were already gutted she wanted to cry. Her pa had never gutted fish for her ma, even though she hated doing it.

"It's a chance I'm willing to take," he answered softly.

Did he have a hidden meaning behind his words or was she imagining things? "How long do you expect winter to last?"

He took off his hat, coat and gloves. "It'll be a good four months or so. Probably more since it started so early. Chigger led those people to their deaths, I'm betting. I looked around to see if I could see anyone else wandering around. Not much going on at all in the woods. No sign of Solomon either. I'm just going to warm up a bit and look in on Ahern. Brian, would you like to go with me to the barn?"

"Yes!"

His excitement gladdened her heart. As she glanced at Patrick, it surprised her to find him studying her. Their gazes locked and it took everything she had to pull her gaze away from him. His eyes mesmerized her somehow and it unsettled her. He'd said his dad was Irish, that's where he probably got his blue eyes. His skin was more of a bronze color, probably from his mother. He carried a great hurt in his heart. Sometimes he'd brood, and she'd see a flicker of anguish in his eyes.

What caused his sadness? She'd never ask. He said he lived up here in the mountains to be away from people. Poor man was stuck with her and Brian. Glancing his way, she blushed. He still stared at her. He raised his left eyebrow and she blushed deeper. There must be something wrong with her. She wasn't some young girl with a crush on a man. She was more the level-headed type who didn't believe in great romance. It was far better to be practical. Surviving and making a life consisted of hard work, not racing hearts and secret glances.

"I found these shears and I think I can use them to cut the deer skin. I hate to ask, but would you put on your other shirt so I can take a look and see how the shirt you're wearing is made?"

She expected a no, but he stood up and took off his shirt. Her jaw dropped. He was all muscle and she'd never seen the like. His shoulders were broad and his chest well-muscled with a sprinkling of dark hair. His stomach was flat with amazing definition. A trail of his dark hair started under his belly button and disappeared under his waistband. Her stomach quivered as she stared. Her gaze traveled upward, taking in his magnificent body. She hadn't realized how much she stared until she reached his face, and he grinned. His head tilted and he cocked his left eyebrow.

She gasped, grabbed his other shirt, and threw it at him. "I don't want you to get cold."

"It seems to have warmed up nicely in here," he responded with a lilt of laughter in his voice.

She wanted to turn away but her feet seemed rooted to the floor. "Brian, get ready to go out and see Patrick's horse. He's warmed up now and can take you."

Patrick threw back his head and laughed loud and deep. "I'm warmed from head to toe, thank ya. Come on, Brian, let's go see Ahern and get supplies to make ya some snowshoes."

"Yes, sir!" Brian was ready and standing at the door in no time.

Patrick was quickly by his side. "Let's go, lad." Before he closed the door behind him, he threw her another grin.

When the door finally closed, she slumped into a chair and covered her burning cheeks with her hands. *Land sakes, what have I gotten myself into?* Closing her eyes she took deep slow breaths to still her erratic heart. He made her feel things she'd never felt before and she didn't like it one bit.

SAMANTHA WAS DOWNRIGHT IGNORING HIM. Since he and Brian returned, she hadn't glanced at him once. She listened intently to Brian while he told her all about Ahern and how to make snowshoes. Smiles were plentiful for the child, but none for him.

Now he remembered why he stayed away from women—they were all crazy. The way she looked at him earlier was most likely curiosity but she scorched his insides. Getting her naked and on his bed became a vision he could not get out of his head. Good thing Brian was around or he'd have scooped her up, put her on his bed, undressed her slowly, and buried himself inside her.

His hands shook slightly as desire ran through his veins. The cabin closed in on him and it was suddenly too small. The sound of horses alerted him, and he quickly grabbed his rifle.

"Get back and try to stay out of sight." Samantha looked stricken and he wished he had the time to reassure her. He opened the door and stepped outside, closing the door firmly behind him.

Utes, four braves and a woman, their horses making a straight line in front of the cabin. It was surprising they'd made it through the snow with the horses. He recognized two of the older ones to be of his mother's band. He never sought them out, but occasionally they would spot each other in the woods.

Patrick nodded. "What brings ya here on such a cold day?"

One of the braves pushed the woman to the ground and she landed with a loud thump, but she didn't cry out.

"Mountain Man, we allowed your mother to go with your father without a bride price. Now it is up to you to pay," the Indian known as Fierce Wind said.

Unease shot up his back. "What do ya mean pay?"

"Violet Flower is no longer welcome in our village. She now belongs to you."

Patrick shook his head. "Wait one minute. What if I don't want to accept your gift?"

Fierce Wind's eyes narrowed. "She will be killed. It is better to end her life than have her wander through the mountains until she dies. By all that is right, she should have her nose cut off and be left to fend for herself. Mountain Man, she is my daughter and now she is yours."

Before Patrick could respond, they turned their horses and rode away, taking the woman's horse with them. She sat in the snow, her eyes lowered and her body shook. He wondered if it was from the cold or being thrown out of her village. He walked toward her and offered his hand. She took his hand and glanced up at him. What a beauty. Her doe eyes and flawless complexion held his gaze. He swallowed hard, helped her up, and walked her into the cabin.

Samantha's expression went from relief to fear. Her eyes widened and she pulled Brian close. It was a reaction he knew but one he never accepted.

"Patrick?" Her voice wavered.

"We have someone else who was left out in the cold. This is Violet Flower and she's, well, she's—"

"I am his woman." Violet Flower took Patrick's hand, tilted her head and smiled at Samantha. "You?"

Samantha's hand flew to her throat. "I'm just someone Patrick rescued. I'm Samantha and this is Brian."

Violet Flower barely acknowledged her. Instead, she wrapped both arms around Patrick and drew their bodies together.

His woman? "It's not true. Her father left her here is all." He pulled away from Violet Flower's embrace and held her shoulders. "Ya are not here as my woman. Ya can stay until the thaw, and then I will see about finding ya a husband."

"What about the baby?" She blinked a few times and frowned.

Patrick's gaze collided with Samantha's unhappy one. He hoped the confusion he felt was obvious for her to see. "What baby?"

Violet Flower took off her robe.

"Wow!" Brian exclaimed. "She's got a really big belly. Is that where babies come from?"

Samantha turned bright red. "It's not polite conversation."

"But—"

"Brian, we can talk about it later." Brian closed his mouth and stared at her with a mulish expression on his face.

Samantha pulled one of the chairs in front of the fire. "Sit and get warm. You must be hungry. I have some biscuits for now and the stew will be ready in a bit." She smiled what she hoped was a reassuring smile, but all she got in return was a deep glare.

Violet Flower waited for a minute and then sat down. She turned toward Patrick. "What about your baby? You would have another raise it?"

Samantha gasped and put the plate of biscuits on the

table. Her hands clasped and she held her breath waiting for Patrick's response.

"Why is it no one tells the truth? I hate lies." He gave Violet Flower a pointed look. "If ya continue to lie I will put ya out. I'm supposin' ya carry a child that is not of your husband. Why else would they send ya away? I know what it means when a woman's nose is cut off."

Brian's eyes grew wide and he stepped closer to Samantha, putting his hand in hers. She gave it a quick squeeze. They watched as Patrick and Violet Flower spoke heatedly in another language.

"Oh, my. Here, eat. I don't think you're supposed to get so upset while you're with child."

Violet Flower took a biscuit from the plate and nodded.

Brian ran and got his coat. "I need to help with Ahern." He quickly scurried out of the cabin.

"You're leaving when the thaw comes?" Violet Flower asked, as she looked Samantha up and down, frowning as though she found her lacking.

"Yes, that's the plan. Patrick found me in the forest. He's a good man." Her face heated at Violet Flower's raised eyebrows.

"He is not your man."

Patrick scowled at them and slammed out the door. He heard Brian scurrying after him.

IN THE BARN, Patrick knelt in front of Brian, strapping the newly made snowshoes onto his falling apart boots. "Lad, ya need to stand still."

Brian stood still for a full thirty seconds before squirming.

"Ya sure are a wriggly one."

"I'm sorry. I'll try to stay still."

Patrick saw the near panic in Brian's eyes. "No need to be afraid around here. No one is going to haul off and hit ya or the like."

Brian nodded but his eyes gave away his unease.

"There, all done. Let's go out and walk on top of the snow." He headed for the door, glancing back making sure Brian was following. "Come on."

Brian hesitantly took a step onto the piled snow and his eyes opened wide. "Look at me! I thought for sure I'd fall right through. I wish I had these when Solomon made me go for firewood and water."

"It's harsh out here in the winter. These shoes help me do what needs doing."

"Like check your traps?"

"Sure, I wouldn't want to take a chance of Ahern getting hurt. I bet Solomon left the mountains for drier ground. Can't get a wagon too far in these snowy mountains."

Brian smiled. "Yeah, I bet he's far, far away."

"Well, I guess we should feed the horse and get back home. It's only getting colder." Brian nodded and followed him into the barn. They made sure Ahern was all settled and made their way to the cabin.

"Can't wait to show Sam my shoes."

"Sam?"

"Well, I can't call her ma so I figured Sam is a good name."

He laughed. "Ya might want to ask her. Women can be a might peculiar when it comes to their names."

Brian nodded and excitedly opened the door. "Look at my snow shoes…"

"What in the blazes?" Patrick roared. Violet Flower stood, knife in hand, cornering Samantha. He quickly disarmed Violet Flower, took her by the arm, and sat her down in the chair. "What do ya think you're doing?" He slammed his hand on the table next to her.

Brian quickly took off his shoes, ran to Samantha's side, and hugged her. She stared at Violet Flower but managed to give him a weak smile. "Everything is fine now." She shook and her white complexion concerned him.

Violet flower sat with her arms crossed glaring at Samantha. He groaned and shook his head. "Ya were going to kill her weren't ya?"

Violet Flower shrugged her shoulders.

"I can't allow ya to stay."

While keeping the Indian woman in his sight, he walked to Samantha and drew her close. She shivered and reached inside his coat, encircling his waist with her arms. It was difficult to keep his face expressionless. He didn't want to add fuel to whatever fight the women were having and he didn't want to put a pregnant woman out into the cold.

"I'm so glad you finally came home. It seemed as though you were gone for hours."

Taking off his gloves, he stroked her back. "I'm here now and I'm grateful I got here in time."

"Yeah, we wouldn't want to try to wash blood off the floor. It ain't an easy thing." Brian sat on the bed swinging his legs back and forth.

From the earnest expression on Brian's face, he figured it was something Brian had done in the past. He'd probably seen far too much for his young years. Closing his eyes, he breathed in her scent; she smelled soap and water clean, not unlike fresh linen on washday. His body started to respond to her and he put a bit of distance between them before she became aware of his need.

"So, Violet Flower, why did you try to slice up Sam?" Brian's voice sounded more curious than mad.

Samantha stepped out of his embrace. "Sam? Slice up?"

"She looked ready to gut ya, Sam. She really did."

"I thought the same thing, Brian." Her voice quavered and Patrick led her to the bed.

"Move over and let your ma, I mean Samantha sit on the bed. I've never seen anyone look so white and not pass out."

Brian scooted over, making room for Patrick to ease her down. He turned and frowned. "I'm not sure what I should do in this situation. This is a small cabin and it's overflowing and busting at the seams. Rightfully I should put ya out, Violet Flower. I really should but I, like your father, wouldn't want ya to suffer out in this weather. On the other hand, I can't have ya threatening anyone in my care. Do ya understand me? We are all strangers to each other and we will learn to get along."

"You will see who the father of this baby is when it is born. Mountain Man, it will probably look more like you." She paused and smiled. "It'll have darker skin, I would guess, since you're half Indian."

"Patrick?" He heard the questions in Samantha's voice. The questions of why didn't you tell me and how did it happen? No one minded when a white man took an Indian for his woman but they took exception to half-breed offspring. It was fine as long as ya kept everything away from the good people of the town. His father wasn't the type to care what others said or did. He didn't care how his wife and son were treated or mistreated. He heard it all in her voice and his stomach sickened. Samantha was like all the rest.

Clenching his jaw, he turned toward her. "Yes, I'm a half breed. And no, I can't take ya somewhere else to stay. It isn't safe to travel but as soon as it is I'll have ya back to your own world."

Her eyes widened as she shook her head. "I didn't—"

"Save it. I've heard it all before." She visibly recoiled and it upset him but he couldn't bear to hear the lies come out of her mouth. "This is how it is going to go. Ya all have to work to earn your keep. Cooking, cleaning, and helping me outside, whatever it takes. I'm not prepared to feed so many but I can and I will, only if there is no more trouble." He glared at Violet Flower. "Don't make me tie ya up to keep the others safe because I will do just that. You're not my woman, that is not my child and I really don't care who the father is since it's none of my business. I will do what I have to, don't test me. If I ever see ya even look at Samantha with your hate-filled eyes ya will suffer. I can always take the baby after it's born and turn ya out."

He heard both women gasp and he didn't know where to look. How had he become the bad guy? It'd been a long time since he'd had to deal with interacting with others. Now, he'd become responsible for three extra people. It was going to be a very long winter.

HER HANDS clasped and unclasped the furs on the bed, while her mind raced. Patrick wasn't such a great man after all. How could a person threaten to take a baby away from a mother? Through the fringe of her eyelashes, she watched him stare into the fire. All was quiet in the log cabin, except for the pounding of her heart. Violet Flower had meant to kill her. She had a vile way of speaking and when she grabbed the knife, Samantha thought it to be all over.

She saw Violet Flower out of the corner of her eye, staring at her. Her hands shook and she became lightheaded. Now was not the time to show weakness but her body betrayed her.

"Sam? You're shaking the bed something awful," Brian said.

Patrick turned and gazed at her with concern in his eyes.

Blood rushed back into her face at his perusal, making her warm, too warm. Pulling her gaze away, she studied her hands, wondering what would happen next. How could she live in the same house with Violet Flower? The woman was sure to try to kill her again.

The chair legs scraped across the floor as Patrick stood. "I'll dish up the stew. Ya look as though ya could use something to eat."

"It's my job. I can do it."

"No. Brian and I will do it for today. A good meal and some rest may help to put us in better moods." Any warmth in his voice had fled and it hurt to see him turn away. It was just as well, they had no future together. He'd made it abundantly clear he couldn't wait for spring to be rid of them all.

"Thank you."

Brian eagerly helped to dish up the stew and bring a plateful to her. He made a wide berth around Violet Flower and she didn't blame him one bit. She knew what it was like being banned and trying to live yet another day, but something had to be done. Somehow, she needed to get through to Violet Flower she didn't have any claim or any plan to claim Patrick.

Dinner was quiet and everyone ate heartily except for a sullen Violet Flower. Too bad, Samantha didn't feel much sympathy for her.

"What will be the sleeping arrangements?"

Patrick ran his fingers through his hair. "That's a tricky one. I had first planned for both ya women to share the bed but that's out of the question now."

"Violet Flower should have the bed since she is in the family way."

"I will not sleep in a bed. I will sleep in front of the fire with Patrick." Violet Flower smiled at her in triumph.

"I'm not sleeping with ya. Take the spot by the fire and I

will sleep on the floor by the bed. I don't trust ya not to slit Samantha's throat while she sleeps."

Samantha gasped and Brian's eyes opened wide. He put his hands on his throat as though protecting it.

"She can sleep in the barn then we could lock the door," Brian offered.

It wouldn't be right to voice her opinion but secretly she agreed with Brian. It was Patrick's cabin and he deserved the respect of following his guidelines. "It's a fine idea, Patrick. I will sleep easier knowing you are so close. I just hope you're not a heavy sleeper."

There was a bit of warmth in Patrick's gaze as he nodded to her. "It'll be fine. Living in the wilderness, a person can't afford to sleep deeply."

"Are you sure ya don't want to bed down with the white woman? I'm used to the ways of a man and his woman."

Heat traveled from her toes to her head. She must be the color of scarlet. Crudeness on this level was new to her and the embarrassment ran deep.

"Good, we won't keep ya from sleeping then."

"You said she's not your woman."

"That's right. I've said it repeatedly but ya refuse to listen. Keep your thoughts to yourself. I don't want to hear them. I think all ya are trying to do is shame Samantha for something she did not do. It is ya who is shamed."

Violet Flower grabbed a small stack of furs and made herself comfortable in front of the fire, turning her back to them.

Samantha sighed and tucked both her and Brian into bed. She watched Patrick as he lay out furs for himself. "Thank you," she whispered.

"For what?"

"For protecting us."

He nodded. "I'm glad I'm good for something." He lay down and turned his back to her.

She lay in the bed as still as possible so not to disturb Brian. What did Patrick mean good for something? She must have missed something but she couldn't figure it out. The events of the day haunted her and she wrapped her arms around her middle to keep from flying apart. As long as Violet Flower thought she was Patrick's woman, she wasn't safe. She'd have to make sure that woman never had reason to think it again.

The next morning a sudden chill woke her. The door stood open and Brian was gone. Her heart pounded as she scrambled out of bed. Patrick was gone as was Violet Flower. *What was going on?* Pulling on her shoes, she chastised herself for sleeping so long and so soundly. She grabbed her useless coat and raced outside. Icy rain pelted her face, stinging her.

Patrick and Brian were gathering as much wood as they could and Violet Flower was tending to Ahern. "What's going on?" Her shout escaped unheard by the wind. No one turned toward her. She tried to reach Patrick but she fell repeatedly until she was too afraid to stand.

When she did finally manage to get his attention, he looked thunderous. He dropped the load of cut wood in his arms and slowly made his way toward her.

"What are ya doing out here? Get back inside before ya hurt yourself."

The forcefulness of his voice caused her to cringe. "I can't get up. It's so icy I keep falling."

Sighing, he whisked her up into his arms and muttering the whole way he brought her inside. He set her down and rubbed his hands up and down her arms. Her whole body tingled at his touch. It pleased and puzzled her at the same time.

"Stay inside. It's dangerous out there and we need to get as much wood inside as we can –ya can't burn wet wood."

Nodding, she watched him go back into the frigid rain. The best thing she could do was make sure they had a hot meal when they came back in. She took off her wet coat and put more wood on the fire. It was not easy to cook over a fire but she had learned during her time on the wagon train. A sharp pain went through her heart. Her parents were sadly missed. It had never occurred to her she'd be without them, yet here she was.

The door opened and Brian came in with an armful of wood. He dropped it just inside the door, without a word turned, and went back outside. Samantha gathered the wood and began to stack it close to the fireplace. It was wet but it would dry. Next Patrick came in and did the same. It became a steady stream of wood piled on the floor and soon she had it stacked up as far as she could reach. One whole wall housed the wood.

She found coffee and put it on for a change then quickly made biscuits. She would have cut slabs of meat to fry but the knives were all missing, and she wondered where Patrick hid them. He seemed worried, very worried. How bad could the storm get?

Violet Flower kicked the door open and walked in carrying two buckets of snow. She set them down and groaned. Quickly Samantha went to the other woman's side and helped her take off her heavy ice-laden coat.

"Come sit by the fire, you must be freezing." She took her hand and led her to the chair nearest the fire. "I'll pour you some coffee." For once Violet Flower wasn't spitting nails at her. In fact, she appeared almost grateful, but Samantha knew better.

"You must know a lot about horses if Patrick allowed you to tend to Ahern."

"Yes, he knows I'm a good woman. Good women know how to please their man."

"I'm sure they do." She handed the other woman a tin cup filled with hot coffee. "This should warm you up."

Violet Flower took the offered drink and quickly wrapped her hands around it.

"You probably shouldn't have been out in this weather."

"I am bearing a child, not an old woman. I do what I'm told. I do what a good helpmate would do. I have the know-how to help Mountain Man in times like these. You don't."

She didn't answer her. She didn't want to take the chance Violet Flower would try to kill her again. Some things were forgivable, but being held at knifepoint pleading for your life wasn't one of them. But Violet Flower was right. She didn't know how to help them survive.

Wind rushed in and swirled around her when Patrick and Brian came inside. They dropped the last of the wood, took off their snowshoes and coats and stacked the wood. Patrick caught her gaze and grinned.

"Good you have coffee ready. Thanks."

"Sit and I'll get it for ya."

"Me too!" Brian told her with a happy grin. "I like coffee too."

Samantha shook her head. "You are too young to drink coffee."

"He did a man's work today. He should drink a man's coffee." Patrick nodded at Brian until Brian smiled even wider.

She opened her mouth and closed it again. Brian needed something warm to drink. Solomon probably let him drink coffee all the time. Taking two cups off the makeshift shelf, she leaned over and grabbed the coffee pot. The heat from the handle scorched her hand, and she cried out.

Patrick rushed to her side, grabbed her hand and plunged

it into one of the buckets of snow. "Ya need to focus on what you're doing," he chided.

"You are too much of a distraction." The words flew out of her mouth.

Patrick rubbed her hand with the snow, wearing a big old grin. "I don't think I've ever been a distraction before. I've been called many things in my life but distraction, hmm. I like it."

She snatched her hand back and turned her back to him. Her face grew painfully red as her body tingled. His masculinity was too much and she acted like a fool. Glancing over her shoulder, she caught Violet Flower narrowing her eyes. Patrick was right, she did need to focus on her task. Otherwise, she might get herself killed.

This time she grabbed a cloth to use for the coffee pot. She poured two cups and put the pot back in the hot coals. "Here you go." Brian thanked her and put the cup against his chest.

Patrick's eyes filled with mirth when she handed him his cup. His intense scrutiny flustered her and her stomach turned flips. Patrick was right, this cabin was too small for them all.

"Aren't ya going to have any?" he asked.

No, I've had mine already." There were only three cups and she wasn't about to make a fuss over something that couldn't be changed. In life, you had to make do.

She grabbed the biscuits, this time protecting her hands, and set the cast-iron pot on the table. "I was going to slice up some meat but—"

"Someone stole the knives." Violet Flower nodded her head toward Patrick.

"It's not stealing if they belong to me. Besides, I didn't want any accidents to happen. I find caution is best."

"You're right. Ya can't steal what's already yours. I do not like the way she looks at you. You are promised to me, Mountain Man. My father said you were honorable and would marry me because of the child. I see he was wrong, you are not honorable." Violet Flower gave him a look of disdain.

Patrick's body stiffened and his lips pressed into a tight line. "Ya know better than to challenge a man's honor. Ya are mean spirited and it's no wonder your man threw ya out."

Samantha gasped and clutched a hand to her pounding chest. "Patrick—"

He waved her away. "No, Samantha. Don't try to make this better. Among the Utes honor is above all else and Violet Flower knows I understand what honor means. For her to question mine is unthinkable. It is something ya never do to a man. I have made sacrifices to be an honorable man, a man of integrity and not the half-breed annoyance the townspeople believe me to be." He paused and took a deep breath. "Violet Flower, I can't condone your lies any longer. Ya are forbidden to speak to me from now on."

"She's forbidden to speak?" Brian frowned.

"She can speak, just not to me." His shoulders dropped as the tension fled his body. At the foot of the bed, he kneeled down and grabbed a locked box from underneath. He drew the key from his boot and unlocked the box. He quickly closed it and Samantha didn't get a glimpse of what was inside except for the knife he retrieved. "Here, Samantha, use this to cook and keep it on ya at all times for protection."

"Pro-- protection? I don't think I could."

"Ya would if ya had to." He strapped on his snowshoes, grabbed his gear and slammed the door on his way out.

Violet Flower stood and slammed her cup onto the wooden table. "You have driven him from his home. You will pay, White Woman."

"You are wrong."

"No! Mountain Man was picked for me to marry. We'd be in bed together sharing ourselves if not for you. You give him no comfort. He sleeps on the floor next to the bed. You have turned him into a senseless man instead of the warrior he is. Once the baby comes, I will be put out. I will be left to starve because of you."

Samantha shook her head. "You have some strange ideas of what is right and what is wrong." She grabbed the empty cups and began to wash them with water she heated over the fire. "There is meanness and anger inside you and I feel sorry for you."

"Sam? Can I go outside?" Brian asked.

"I think Patrick needs time alone to think. It's best you stay here. Do you know how to read?"

Brian shook his head.

"We can get started in a minute. We may not have a slate but we have the hearth and ashes. It'll do just fine."

"I don't go much for learnin' and the like."

"It'll be fun and it will help to pass the time." She smiled at the doubt he showed. It would help to pass the time and she needed something to do besides banter with the other woman.

It was warm sitting near the fire. She patted a place next to her for Brian to sit. "It'll be fun, I promise."

He frowned at her and hesitated but he finally sat next to her. It would be an uphill battle but she hoped to make learning fun.

Smoothing out a good amount of white ash on the ground before them, she grabbed a stick. A few of the mothers on the wagon train had taught their children in the same manner. "This is the first letter." She drew a capital A in the ashes and then handed the stick to Brian. "You try."

Brian took the stick and pressed his tongue against his

top lip as though he pondered the fate of the world. He made a perfect letter A and smiled. "I did it!"

The other woman snorted and shook her head.

Samantha shrugged. She wasn't going to let Violet Flower ruin her good mood. "Let's try another."

Brian nodded eagerly. He was a quick learner and took pride in each letter he wrote. Every time he smiled in satisfaction, Violet Flower snorted or sniffed. One time she actually growled.

"Do you know how to make clothes from buckskin?" Samantha asked.

"Of course I do, but I'm not making clothes for you."

She wanted to roll her eyes at her but tried for a serene expression instead. "Patrick needs a shirt and a pair of pants."

"For Mountain Man I will make a set of buckskins." Her eyes gleamed as though she'd won a battle but she had no idea she was doing exactly what Samantha wanted—to be shown how to make clothes from the deer skins.

Patrick came in from the cold and quickly glanced around. He probably expected trouble. He took off his coat, hat, and gloves then unstrapped his snowshoes. He started toward the fire and Brian shrugged.

"Sam wanted to pass the time showing me some learning. Men like us don't need learning do we?"

Disappointment flashed through Samantha. She'd thought they'd had fun. She stared up at Patrick and he cocked his left brow as he stared back. "Actually men like us do need to be educated. Too many people in the world try to take advantage of others. It's a good thing to know how to read and do some figuring too."

The wide grin on her face wouldn't vanish no matter how hard she tried. Her heart filled with pride for Patrick. He really was a good man. Not because he could read, but because he saw things as they were and took steps to make sure he didn't come out the loser.

Brian nodded happily. He'd enjoyed learning and she was surprised at how much Patrick's approval meant to him.

"I'm glad you're in out of that bitter cold. I'm also sorry if we drove you to leave your own house. You're right, the cabin is too small for bickering." She started to stand and Patrick gently took her arm and helped her. His nearness made her heart flutter so she instantly stepped away.

"I nearly forgot I brought ya something."

"You brought the white woman something?"

"It's for all of us." Patrick shook his head and mumbled. He walked to the door, opened it and grabbed two crates from outside. "We can sit on these so we can all eat together."

"It's a wonderful idea, Patrick." Samantha tried one out. "It's the perfect height for the table."

"Good."

"I'm going to make you new buckskins to wear. I know how." Violet Flower raised her chin in pride.

Samantha wasn't sure he'd answer.

Patrick smiled at her. "Thank ya."

She closed her eyes and prayed for peace, hoping it wasn't too much to ask.

CHAPTER FOUR

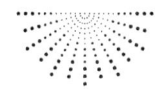

Patrick gazed up at the cloudless sky. He lit his pipe and took a deep draw. He knew what cabin fever meant. He'd never minded the mountain winters before, but this year, hell, any excuse to be outside became a blessing. In the last two weeks, every day played out the same. Samantha did all the housework and Violet Flower sat making him his buckskins, all the while glaring.

Samantha ignored her for the most part, which was for the best, and Brian was learning words. Perhaps the next time he was in town he'd buy a book for the boy. He took the pipe out of his mouth and shook his head. What was he thinking? They'd be gone by the next time he went into town or at the very least, they'd go to town with him and part ways.

There was no doubt in his mind— Samantha would take Brian with her back East. At least he thought she was going back East—it was the only thing that made sense. As for Violet Flower, there were other bands of Utes besides the Mountain Utes. He'd have to do it before the council gathering or word would get out about her unfaithfulness.

By the size of her belly, he guessed her time would be soon. He relaxed a bit, knowing she was unwieldy and less likely to kill anyone. Samantha knew how to deliver a baby, didn't she? All women probably knew. He planned to take Brian for a walk while it took place.

Puffing on his pipe, his thoughts drifted to Samantha. In fact, it was too common an occurrence, but he couldn't help himself. She was a truly kind woman and too good for him. He knew the rules, society's rule, and he couldn't have her. There was no way he'd subject her to being ostracized because of him. A hurt ran to the very core of him, one he would never completely shake. No, it was not a life for her.

Additional snow had fallen in the last few weeks, covering the ice. It was time for him to scout around. There were many ice and snow-laden branches felled or close to falling and he'd need to clear the area of the possible dangers. A big branch falling on Brian could kill him. Emptying his pipe, he then slid it into his pocket. He went into the barn, greeted Ahern, grabbed his axe and started clearing a safe path toward one of his traps.

It was hard work keeping an eye on the branches above while watching where he walked. He dragged heavy tree limbs to the side of the path and chopped down ones he could reach. Eventually he'd drag the wood back to the cabin to use for the fire.

He made his way down to the river where he'd laid a trap. Looking up one way and down the other, he couldn't believe his trap was gone. Traps weren't cheap but he did end up losing at least one a year. It was probably in the river. Slogging on, he reached the next trap, or rather where the trap was supposed to be. His brow furrowed and he made sure he was in the right place. He squatted down and inspected the area. He wiped away snow from the area and sure enough in the ice-packed snow underneath was a boot print.

A white man and a stranger. A trapper would rather starve than steal a trap. There were unspoken rules in the mountains. Troubled, he made his way to the cabin, dragging one of the downed branches with him. Someone was in these woods and he needed to protect both women and Brian. Did Samantha know how to use a rifle? Shaking his head, he smiled. She was full of surprises. She just might know how to shoot.

The snapping of a twig on the ground alerted him he wasn't alone. He dropped the branch and sidestepped off the path into the dense woods. He stood behind a tree, listening and waiting. All was quiet but he could sense someone was out there. Ducking, he silently made his way up the mountain away from the cabin. He stopped frequently, scanned the area, and listened. Stopping behind a few downed trees, he watched and waited.

Finally, he grabbed a branch and did his best to wipe away his shoe prints from the snow. A real tracker wouldn't be fooled. It was hard to wipe away tracks in the snow. He laid tracks going in various directions and headed back to the cabin. Who was this person and how were they surviving in this weather? Damn, maybe Smitty died. He hadn't looked well the last time he saw him. He'd check it out tomorrow.

Once the cabin was in sight, he breathed a sigh of relief until he got closer. One of his missing traps was set right outside the cabin door. He quickly made his way to it and stuck the branch he'd been using into the trap and added a bit of weight. The jaws of the trap closed and snapped the end of the branch off. The pounding of his heart echoed in his ears. He'd have to track down the son of a bitch and soon.

The cabin door opened and Samantha stuck her head out. Her eyes lit up. "I thought I heard something."

"Grab your coat. I need to talk to ya."

She stared at him as though she was trying to read his

mind. Nodding, she closed the door. When the door opened, again she was dressed for the outdoors. "What's wrong?"

He nodded his head in the direction of the trap.

"I don't understand."

Grabbing her hand, he led her into the barn and closed the door. Her breathing sounded labored. "I shouldn't have dragged ya like that. I know the snow is deep. We have a problem. That trap was set and laid right outside the cabin door. I just found it."

She covered her mouth with her hand.

"Two of my traps are missing and someone was out there in the woods. I thought I led him away from the cabin but he was here. I need to go. I have to find this animal before he ends up harming anyone."

"Are you going now?"

"Yes, I can try to track him while the signs are still fresh and there is no new snow to cover them. I'll need food to take with me. I probably won't be home for a few days. I have a good idea where he's been holed up."

"You could get hurt." Her eyes filled with worry and his heart flipped.

"I protect those under my care. It'll be fine. Do ya know how to shoot a rifle?"

Her eyes widened and she nodded. "You don't think I'll have to shoot anyone, do you?"

He took off his glove and touched the side of her face. Her skin was so soft under his fingers. He stroked her cheek with the pad of his thumb. "No. I'm just glad ya know how to shoot. The shotgun is hidden under the mattress on top of the ropes. Now, the shells are in the wooden clock on the mantle."

"Is that why the clock doesn't work?"

He smiled. "I don't need a clock, and I figure if someone broke into my place they wouldn't want a broken clock."

"Please be careful."

Her sweet voiced pulled him in but he fought the urge to kiss her. "I need ya to get me the food. I don't want to go into the cabin and get everyone worried. Just tell them I'm going hunting and may spend the night with an old trapper friend." She was so damn beautiful. He dropped his hand.

"Okay. I'll get food for you. Do you need anything else?"

Sweet Lord, she didn't know what she was asking. "No, the food will be fine. I have everything else I need." She walked away while his body screamed for her to return. "You're lucky, Ahern, ya don't have a temptation so powerful ya think ya'll lose control." He stroked the horse's neck.

He didn't have to wait long before Samantha, shivering from the cold, returned.

"I hope this will do. Canned beans and biscuits. I could make you something…"

"This is more than enough, thank ya." He took the offered sack and his gaze lingered on her sweet lips. He met her gaze and the way she looked at him made his heart flutter. The sack fell out of his grasp as he took a step forward, cupped the back of her head and took her lips with his. She reached up and wrapped her arms around him and he stilled. He had to walk away but she tasted of everything good. He coaxed her mouth open and almost smiled against her lips when she gasped. He deepened the kiss, promising himself this would be the one and only kiss they would ever share.

The feeling of finally finding his place in the world intoxicated him, and her lips were so soft, so giving. Reluctantly he pulled away and pressed his forehead against hers, trying to regain his center. She moved until their gazes met and he groaned. Her eyes held promises he couldn't accept.

"I have to go."

"I know. Be safe."

He grabbed his belongings and walked out of the barn. He

turned to have one last look and saw her face aglow, with her fingers slightly touching her lips. He'd never really known happiness until now. It was just as well there would be a bit of distance between them.

Samantha tingled from a rush of pleasure she'd never experienced before. One kiss could do that? She glowed when he turned and gave her one last glance. Finally he was just a speck in the lush woods, then gone. Did he feel the same way about her?

It had been so hard to pretend indifference to him but she did what she had to. Violet Flower still glared at her. The last two weeks cooped up with her had gotten on her last nerve. Without privacy, she couldn't wash herself properly.

At least now, she could give Brian a bath and take one herself. Violet Flower, how'd she get such a pretty name? Her name should be Stink Weed. A wide grin spread across her face. From now on whenever she said Violet Flower she would think Stink Weed. A private joke would help the tension a whole lot. She'd hoped Stink Weed would have become nicer as her time neared. It was a false hope. In fact, she was ornery and believed her needs came first. She demanded the first helping at each meal, the first cup of coffee or tea and she refused to turn her back while others changed clothes or tried to wash up. Patrick hung a blanket when needed for privacy but it wasn't quite adequate.

Jamming her hands into her pockets, she trudged through the snow, back to the cabin. She opened the door and gasped. Brian had his back to the fire and was precariously close to the flames. In two quick strides, she reached him and pulled him away from the fire. "Are you alright?"

He gave her a strange look. "What's wrong?"

"Did you feel the fire hot on your back?"

He shrugged. "I felt nice and warm."

She turned him toward the fire. "Look where you were sitting and how close the flames were to you."

His eyes widened. "Wow, I need to be more careful."

Hugging him to her she nodded, her throat too closed to answer.

"You need to watch him," Violet Flower said, her voice sarcastic.

"Thanks for your help," she shot back. She turned away before she said something she'd later regret.

She fussed over Brian for a bit, trying to regain her equilibrium. Patrick's kiss had put her off balance. She touched her lips and smiled. Immediately she realized her mistake as Stink Weed gave her a piercing, knowing look.

"Just remember Mountain Man is mine," she hissed.

Samantha turned away and closed her eyes, praying for patience. "Since Patrick will probably be gone all night, I think it'll be bath night."

"Aww, Sam."

"I know you have no love for bathing, but it will be easier with less people to trip over in here. Violet Flower what about you?" She didn't bother to turn to the woman. She didn't expect an answer.

"I would like to, only if no one sees me."

A spiteful reply almost passed her lips and Samantha swallowed. "Fine."

Brian searched her gaze with widened eyes and she shrugged at him. She knew very well his discomfort of Violet Flower's refusal to give others privacy. It was near the other woman's time and she wanted her clean for the birth. It would be safer, at least she hoped so. Her mother always kept store with the philosophy of cleanliness being the best way to heal.

"After we eat, we can begin our baths. I think we can all use privacy tonight." She glanced over her shoulder at Stink Weed, hoping she got the message.

"I want to take my bath first."

"Of course you do." Ignoring Violet Flower, she got their meal together and they ate. Brian regaled her with his imaginings of what Patrick might be doing. Her only wish was for his safe return.

After they finished she pulled the wash tub in front of the fire and poured a bucket of hot water in it. Next, she poured some cold water in. Taking a bar of lye soap and a fresh towel, she handed them to Violet Flower. "Here you go. We will turn our backs." Instantly she wondered if turning their backs to her was such a good idea. Brian sat at the table facing the front door. She sat next to him, her body tense and ready to react if need be.

All was silent. "Do you need help?"

A reluctant yes was given in reply and Samantha stood and turned. Lord help her, but she wanted to laugh. Violet Flower was stuck in her dress.

"Hold on and let me help. It must be hard in your condition." It took a bit of doing, Violet Flower was much taller than she was but she managed to get her clothes off without looking.

"Thank you."

Surprised, she looked at her and gasped. There were thin lashes on her sides and she suspected her back was lined. "Do they-- do they hurt? Let me check your back."

Jutting out her chin, Violet Flower shook her head. "No. It is my business. Please go sit down."

Opening her mouth to speak, she quickly closed it and nodded. It wasn't her business and if the whip marks were infected, they would have known by now. Her heart went out to the cantankerous woman. She actually knew little about her. She sat back down next to Brian and they spelled out words aloud.

When Violet Flower was finished, Samantha helped her dress, led her to a chair Brian put in front of the fire and wrapped her up in a fur. "I have coffee on for you. It will be ready soon. Brian, come and help me empty the water from the tub."

Brian grumbled, but he helped her. Next, she made Brian take a bath, the world's quickest bath, and then she took one herself. The water felt wonderful and to her surprise, Violet Flower didn't look. Perhaps the woman had reason to be so hostile, not that she was excusing her behavior, but maybe she understood it.

The dark silence of the night covered them as they lay to sleep but sleep eluded her. Now was time for reflection and the kiss she'd shared with Patrick whirled in her thoughts. Where she came from a kiss meant something. It meant intentions leading to marriage. Her heart dropped. It probably meant nothing to Patrick. Why would it? Women were most likely plentiful for him. If he'd wanted a wife, he'd have one—wouldn't he? After all, he was very handsome and strong. He could provide well for a family. Turning on her side, she watched the flames twist and turn. It was probably how warped Violet Flower's heart was, if she even had one. Maybe she wasn't being fair. They were just a group of people who had no one.

PATRICK STARED at the old log cabin. There was no fire but tracks led to it. His suspicion Smitty was dead was probably right. The wind howled through the trees as he made his way to the back of the cabin. He backed further into the woods, into the shadow of the trees. He'd hunker down and wait until morning. He'd survived colder temperatures before. Sitting down, he leaned his back against the trunk of a massive fir tree, placing his rifle across his lap.

People thought Indians were the ones to fear. He'd always had fair dealings with them. The white men came and made trouble. This was one man he was itching to pummel. They'd played a game of hide and seek all afternoon. The other man knew he was being followed and was amazingly adept at hiding his tracks. These were his woods and he eventually found the trail.

Thoughts of Samantha kept him company. Her skin so soft, so white, was the problem. He never should have kissed her. It only ignited a bigger need for her and there would be no happy ending. Her fascination with him came from him being different and that same fascination would hurt her. Damn, she felt so good in his arms. There was a sense of peace when he kissed her, along with unquenchable desire. She stirred him like no other. Sighing, he looked up at the moon, wondering if they were all getting along. Maybe it was a good thing to have Brian and Violet Flower as chaperones. Although there were plenty of times he wished the opposite.

Her soft lips—a lighted match caught his attention. Must be too cold in the cabin for the polecat. He shook his head. Being a trapper was not the life for everyone. Hell, only a few stuck with it after one winter. He enjoyed the solitude, or so he thought until Samantha came along.

He watched and waited until the sun came up. He made his way to the front of the cabin, being careful not to be seen. He wanted a good look at the coward who left a set trap for the women and Brian. He took another step and he didn't have time to react before the jaws of the trap clamped painfully around his ankle. The pain was unbearable but he didn't cry out.

The front door opened and a tall, slender man came out.

Patrick knew the man couldn't see him, but he stared his way. Was that Solomon? He aimed his rifle but the weasel was quicker. He shot the rifle out of his hands and laughed.

"How does it feel to be caught in your own trap?"

"I take it you're Solomon? What kind of game are you playing?"

"Yes, I'm Solomon. The game is called getting even. You stole from me, so I'm stealing from you. You made life hard for me so I'm trying to make it miserable for you."

"So, taking my pelts and traps weren't enough for ya?" he growled.

"I want what is mine." Solomon smirked. "And for my trouble I think I'll help myself to what isn't mine. She's a pretty little thing. I bet she'd be willing to go with me. I can't imagine her staying with a half-breed like you."

Patrick tried to keep his expression calm. He'd dealt with men like this before, men who feed off the fear of others. No, he wouldn't give him the satisfaction. Solomon didn't step close enough for him to grab and Patrick had the feeling he'd be shot down if he tried to escape the trap.

Solomon made a wide circle around him to get to the tree. The trap was affixed to the tree by a chain and lock. Giving it a hard yank, he laughed as Patrick fell. "Well I won't have to worry about you trailing me today. Don't think I'll be back this way. I just might hole up at your place, seeing as you won't need it anymore."

Patrick glared but stayed silent as he lay on the cold ground. He wanted Solomon to be confident in his plan as he left. He wouldn't look over his shoulder if he wasn't expecting anyone to be there and it would be a great advantage.

Solomon went inside, grabbed his stuff and walked away on Smitty's snowshoes.

Poor bastard. He hoped Smitty had died before Solomon

came across him. He could feel blood seep down his leg but he remained still. He waited to see if Solomon would double back. Slowly he got up, groaning the whole while. Bending down, he drew the sides of the trap down as he lifted his weight off. Many men couldn't do it but most trappers could. It was survival in the mountains.

He rummaged through his stuff until he found an old length of cloth he carried for such emergencies. Lifting his pant leg, he grimaced and tied the cloth around his wounds. Damn, figures it was his best bear trap. The bone wasn't broken and that was all that mattered. When he was done, he looked up at the sky, Solomon only had an hour lead-time on him.

His mountain, his trails. If Solomon was so big on traps, he'd set one just for him.

SAMANTHA WATCHED outside as Brian brought in more wood. She stared at the place she last saw Patrick, hoping he'd suddenly appear. "I think we need to tend to Ahern," she called to him. Brian nodded as he went inside, his arms laden with logs. She loved the change in him; he now trusted her.

Shuddering as a blast of cold air came her way, she hurried into the barn. A wide grin graced her face at the sight of Ahern. She'd been around horses before, but none as noble looking as the one she petted. "I miss Patrick too," she murmured.

"Too bad since he ain't coming back."

She turned toward the menacing voice and gasped. "Who--who are you?"

"Does it really matter, Samantha?"

How did he know her name? "You said Patrick isn't coming back?" She slowly inched toward the door.

"If he ain't dead now, he will be soon. Poor fellow got caught in his own trap." His sinister smile sickened her.

Out of the corner of her eye, she spotted Brian running her way. "Don't come in here!" she shouted. Her heart was in her throat as he came barreling in.

He stopped short and shook his head. "Solomon, how did you find me?" His voice wavered.

"Well now, you don't think I'd let my best buddy freeze in these mountains, do you? I've been looking for you. In fact, it's cost me a lot of time and effort to rescue you."

Brian stiffened and his eyes grew wide. There was no hiding the stark fear on his face.

"Brian, run! Find Patrick, he's in trouble."

Brian hesitated and gave her a long look before he took off like a rabbit across the clearing.

Solomon roared and pushed her to the ground before he chased after Brian. Getting up, she raced into the cabin and grabbed the rifle.

"What is happening?"

"Stay here, Violet Flower. A man named Solomon is after Brian and he said Patrick was dying." Her hands shook as she checked to be sure the rifle was loaded. She knocked the old clock to the ground, grabbed more shells and shoved them into her pocket. Sprinting to the door, she pulled it open, only to find the tall man on the other side ready for her. He grabbed the rifle and hit her in the head with the butt of it. Everything went black.

Her eyes fluttered and her hand touched her head as she groaned. *What happened?* She remembered and suddenly sat up. The room seemed to tilt one way then the other. After scanning the cabin, she sighed, relieved Brian was not there. Maybe Solomon would just leave.

"My, my look who's awake. I was getting a bit worried that I might have hit you too hard." He sat in one of the chairs, placed in front of the door, with his rifle cradled in his arms. His coonskin hat was on the table and his long, stringy, filthy hair was in view.

Cringing, her gaze met Violet Flower's. There might have been a hint of fear in her eyes but it was hard to tell. Her face was as stoic as usual. Disappointed, she looked away. She'd hoped for a look of comradery. Something to give her a signal they were on the same side.

"Flower, put more wood on the fire, I'm cold." He barked and when she hesitated, he stood and took a step toward her. "There are other ways I can keep warm and you well know it."

Violet Flower immediately stood and put two more logs to burn. Her mouth formed a grim line. Had she known Solomon before? Something wasn't right, but what could be right in such a situation?

"Then again maybe a white woman would give me more satisfaction. What do you think, Flower?" He smirked at them both.

"Maybe she would."

Samantha gasped and her hand went to her throat. Maybe she would? What type of response was that? Obviously, it was each woman for herself. Closing her shaking hands, she kept her gaze on them, hoping Solomon would forget her. She said a brief prayer for Brian and Patrick's safety. Her heart dropped as she remembered what the man had said about Patrick being dead or near death. It couldn't be true, it just couldn't.

"Hope that little brat returns home soon. I'd hate to have to go after him now that I've found him."

"You've been in these mountains the whole time? Where did you stay?"

"Some old geezer was kind enough to croak so I could

have a warm place. I like it here better." He licked his lips. "The scenery is much better, right Flower?"

Samantha's eyes narrowed. "You two know each other."

"We sure do, don't we Flower? You see, me and Flower here have a special relationship. I find her in the woods and she spreads her legs for me. Right, Flower?"

The roiling of her stomach was almost too much. "Violet Flower doesn't seem the type to allow anyone to do anything like that to her."

"She's married, you know. I got her once and the threat of telling her warrior husband about us kept her mine. She hadn't been around lately and her husband has a new wife already. Pretty little thing."

Violet Flower had remained calm until the last part about her husband was said. Suddenly she lunged at Solomon with a knife in her hand. A shot rang out and Violet Flower sank to the ground, blood pouring from her shoulder.

Samantha quickly stood but stilled when the rifle was pointed at her. "I just want to help her is all. She's bleeding something awful."

"Do you have a knife too?"

"Y, yes. The one I use to cook with. Actually no."

"Which is it?"

She shook at his gruff voice. "Violet Flower must have stolen the knife while I was in the barn."

"You ain't too smart, are ya? Get over here and patch her up. She's carrying my baby and I'm not sure if I want it or not."

Disgust filled her as she grabbed a towel and scurried over to Violet Flower's side, pressing the towel against her shoulder to staunch the bleeding. It took a bit of doing but she got it to slow.

"Put the knife in the fire," Solomon demanded.

"Why?"

"Don't ask questions, just do it."

She stared at him for a moment then moved just close enough to him to grab the knife. There was no doubt in her mind, he'd shoot her if she disobeyed. "In the fire?"

"Just the blade. You'll have to seal up the bullet holes in her with the knife."

"I see." She really didn't see. Sounded painful to her.

"The baby," Violet Flower croaked.

Putting the knife in the fire, she instantly went to Violet Flower's side. "Let me help you to the bed."

Violet flower shook her head vehemently. "No bed."

Nodding, she took a few clean furs and laid the biggest one on the floor. It looked to be in the shape of a bear. What if Brian met up with a bear? Helping the other woman, she laid her on the fur. This wasn't her first baby. She'd helped with two while she was on the wagon train. "I need to boil water."

"Do what you need, just remember I'm watching you."

Samantha nodded and put water on to heat. She grabbed a piece of the leather stripping Violet Flower had used to stitch the buckskins together. She'd need it to tie off the baby. Violet Flower neither writhed nor screamed and she began to wonder if she was really in labor. "Are you okay?"

"Indian women don't carry on like your kind does." Solomon told her. "I think the knife is hot enough."

"You don't expect me—"

"Hell you have no backbone, do ya? Go sit on the bed until I'm done."

She backed away until the back of her knees hit the bed and she immediately sat down. As soon as she saw the glow of the hot knife, she closed her eyes. The searing sound then the smell of burnt flesh made her gag. Her body tensed. He still had to do the back of Violet Flower's shoulder. Once again, she heard the searing of the hot knife on flesh. This time she opened her eyes and the sheer pleasure on Solomon's face frightened her. How could he be so evil? She shivered doubly glad Brian had escaped.

"There all done, now get on with birthing that baby."

Back by Violet Flower's side, she bathed her brow with cool water. "You didn't even utter a sound."

Solomon laughed maliciously. "That's why I like her. She never cries out."

She ignored him and concentrated on trying to make the other woman comfortable. "I'm surprised you didn't pass out. You are a very brave and strong woman."

Violet Flower's eyes widened and softened. "Thank you, so are you."

The words both surprised and warmed her. They'd been on opposite sides of a silent feud for months now. She wasn't sure of the outcome but she hoped she could count on Violet Flower's hate for Solomon to help them both. What did Solomon mean about not deciding about the baby yet? Did he mean to take it with him?

Violet Flower began to pant and she took it as sign things were moving along with the birth. She positioned herself to have a look. "You're crowning. It won't be long now."

Violet Flower nodded, exhaustion written all over her face. "The clothes I made for the baby…"

"I'll get them. Hold on." She'd watched her fashion baby clothes out of deerskin for a while now but she never really saw what she made. The fur-lined buckskins were plentiful and she grabbed a couple. A baby swaddled in one of these would be very warm indeed. Returning to Violet Flower, she got ready. "That's it, one shoulder, yes, now the other. Push!"

She grabbed the baby, tied off the umbilical cord and used the knife to cut it. Next, she used warm water to bathe the crying child and eventually she laid the baby on Violet Flower for inspection.

"It's a girl," Violet Flower said, her voice full of wonder.

"She's beautiful. Look at all the dark hair she has already. Lay still while I tend you." She draped one of the fur-lined skins over the baby and tended to the new mother. The whole birthing and Solomon holding them captive tired her but she needed to be alert for any chance of escape, though she doubted Violet Flower could get far for a few days.

"Out of the way! I want to see the baby." Solomon pushed her until she fell back on her bottom. He pulled the covering off and stared at the baby. "A useless good for nothing girl. I might as well put her out into the snow. I have no need for her."

"You're a beast!" Solomon slapped her face with his open hand. Gingerly Samantha touched her throbbing cheek and said nothing more.

Solomon went back to his chair in front of the door. "She does look like a half breed. She might be good to sell in a few years. I'll have to think on it. No sense being hasty now, is there? I heard tell men like girls who aren't all Indian. A nice half-and-half female could pay off after all."

Samantha's stomach tightened as her heart dropped. What type of evil was she dealing with? Never in her life had she encountered such a thing. Growing up, everyone was kind. It wasn't until she was banned from the wagon train that she experienced the other side of people. Then there was Chigger leading those people to probable death in greed. Now Solomon.

"Will you lie in the bed? You can sit up, lean against the wall and admire your pretty girl."

Violet started to shake her head, and then stopped. "I'll give it a try."

Smiling, she reached down and gently took the baby in her arms. She placed her on the bed and went back to help

Violet Flower to the bed. After she got both mother and daughter tucked in, she began to clean up the cabin.

"I need to bury the afterbirth and the bloody towels. I also want to dump the dirty water."

He grunted at her, looked her up and down and finally nodded. "If you don't return, the baby dies. I'll throw it into the fire."

Chills racked her as she gulped. "I'll be right back. I'll stay in sight of the cabin. It might take some doing, digging into the frozen ground."

She put on Violet Flower's warm coat and went outside, wishing there was something she could do but she didn't dare take a chance. She wholly believed he'd throw the baby in the fire and laugh while doing it. She dumped the warm water and it melted a bit of the snow. Next, she grabbed a shovel from the barn and began to dig. By the time she finished her hands were frozen and blistered. She put her hands in the coat pockets and felt a knife. Her lips twitched. Violet Flower was full of surprises. She glanced at the front door before slipping the knife into her shoe.

Next, she filled the bucket with snow and used her hands to clean it out. It wasn't even close to having water but it worked. Filling the bucket with clean snow, she stood up and started for the cabin. Out of the corner of her eye, she saw movement and before she could turn her head, Solomon opened the door.

"Get yourself in here! You've had enough time out there."

"I'm coming." She pretended to stumble and then she fell, laying with her head in the direction she saw the movement in the woods. Slowly she pushed herself up and Patrick showed himself. Her heart beat out of her chest, and she wished she could cry out and run into his safe arms but she couldn't risk it.

Solomon grumbled and took a step outside. She held her

breath, afraid he'd see Patrick. Her fear came to life as Solomon lifted his rifle in Patrick's direction. Before she could scream, an arrow flew through the air and pierced Solomon in the chest. He clutched at it in surprise and sank to the ground.

Standing, she became glued to her spot. All she could do was stare at Solomon. Suddenly she snapped out of it and began to run toward the cabin. *Indians*. She grabbed the rifle from the ground and turned scanning the clearing. Where were they? What about Patrick? Did they find Brian out there?

She cocked the weapon ready to shoot.

"Whoa, love. It's me and Brian and a few friends." Patrick awkwardly hurried toward her with Brian right behind. She held the rifle tight, ready to defend them all.

"It's all right. It's me."

Blinking she stared at him. "You're limping." Her mind whirled with questions and she didn't know where to begin. "Brian?"

"Right here, Sam."

Patrick eased the gun from her. "It's fine. Everything will be fine."

"Indians," she whispered.

"Yes, they are my friends."

"Oh." She started to sag and Patrick easily picked her up and brought her inside the cabin.

THANK GOD, she was alive. He carried her into the house, worried and relieved at the same time. He didn't anticipate the new addition to his household to have arrived so soon. He couldn't help but smile at the serene picture Violet Flower and her baby painted. Was that a smile on her face?

"Is Sam okay?"

"Scoot over so I can lay her down next to ya. I think she fainted or something." Did Violet Flower just call Samantha Sam? What happened to White Woman?

"I'm fine," Samantha protested, struggling to get into a sitting position. "Where is Brian?" Her voice quavered.

"I'm right here, Sam. I'm a hero, you know. I saved Patrick all by myself and I led the Utes back to the cabin." His shoulders straightened, as he stood straight and tall.

Samantha smiled at Brian and she relaxed her tense body. "Of course you're a hero. I've always known you were special."

Brian's face glowed at her praise.

"My band is outside?" Violet Flower held her baby closer as her eyes widened in fear. "They want to take my baby away."

"I don't think that's why they're here, Violet Flower. In fact, your husband, Charging Bear was on his way here. I'll let him explain why."

She huddled against the wall. "He will kill my baby girl." Tears threatened to spill.

Samantha reached out and put her hand on his forearm. "You can't allow anyone to take the baby away." Her eyes pleaded with him.

Squeezing her small hand, he smiled. "Her husband wants her back. He knows the truth of what happened. I guess there was a witness. It was her father who insisted she leave."

Samantha shook her head. "She has whip scars on her back. We can't send her back."

Violet Flower moved closer to Samantha. "The whipping was from my father, not my husband. I would like to see him."

He wondered what went on in the last twenty-four hours. Why were they so friendly to one another and who softened

Violet Flower's demanding ways? He didn't dare ask. Peace was a good thing. "Are ya both okay? Solomon didn't—."

Samantha reached out her hand and he helped her up. "We were too busy with the baby and all. I'm just glad he's dead." She walked over to Brian and put her arms around him. "Thank you for all your help."

Brian seemed decidedly uncomfortable with her affection.

Patrick nodded at Violet Flower. "She's a beautiful baby. We'll wait outside and let your husband have a moment alone with ya."

"He will laugh when he sees me in a bed."

"Maybe. We'll be right outside if ya need us." He grabbed Samantha's coat and helped her put it on. "Let's go."

Solomon's body had already been dragged away. "Ya can go in now. She wants to see ya."

The man whose horse was in front of the others nodded then jumped down. Charging Bear touched Brian's head as he passed and he hurried into the cabin.

"Violet Flower will be fine, won't she?" Samantha stared up at him.

"She will." He gave her a quick grin of reassurance. "He loves her."

"Why did she keep saying the baby was yours?"

"I guess she was desperate. The father was white so she probably figured people would believe her." He shrugged and shook his head. A gust of wind kicked up, causing her to shiver. Instinctively he took her hands and pulled her toward him, opening his coat enough for her to fit inside too. Her initial surprise turned into laughter.

"I always feel like a newborn kitten when you do this."

"What's wrong with wanting ya warm?" He hugged and relished the smell of her. Her hair smelled soap and water clean. "Was the birth an easy one?"

"Depends what you call easy. She was shot in the shoulder, then her wounds were seared closed with a red-hot knife. The baby was the easy part. She is a very strong woman and very brave."

"There seems to be friendliness between ya two."

"I guess you could say that." Her arms went around his waist, bringing her body flush against his. He wondered if she could feel his arousal.

"Brian found me stumbling out in the woods and as we walked back home we ran into our guests. The same woman who told Charging Bear that Violet Flower was unfaithful finally admitted Violet Flower wasn't willing."

She shivered against him. "Solomon forced Violet Flower many times. It's his baby."

He rested his cheek against her soft hair. "She knew the baby would be half white. Now I know why she insisted it was mine. Life can be hell for an Indian woman alone with a half-breed child." He couldn't hide his bitterness.

"It was hard for you." She hugged him tighter until his throat clogged. No one had understood or cared before.

Charging Bear walked out of the cabin, a big grin crossed his face. His expression was one of sheer pride. "I have a daughter." His friends all congratulated him. He gazed at Patrick and gave him a nod of thanks. "I'm willing to take the other boy too. He will make a fine warrior."

Samantha pulled away and before he could stop her, she stood toe to toe with Violet Flower's husband. "You are not to lay one finger on Brian. He will be staying with me."

"You're not his family."

Her eyes widened. "Neither are you. I want him with me. I will take care of him."

He smirked. "You and Mountain Man will raise him together? Help him grow into a great man?"

"No, I, we, I can raise him myself." She folded her arms in front of her and lifted her chin.

"What do you say, Mountain Man? You taking these two on?"

His heart raced in panic. Samantha wouldn't want to stay with him and it wasn't fair to the boy. He was about to say no when he met her pleading gaze. He'd come to regret it, he just knew it but… "Yes, I'm taking them on."

Brian gave a big whoop and ran toward him, almost knocking him back with an eager hug. "Thank you."

Patrick patted him on the back, not knowing what to say. Samantha strode toward them and her smile both warmed him and filled him with apprehension. He'd let her have her happiness for now, until they talked. It was for the best he take them to town in the spring and leave them. He just hoped it wouldn't be as hard as he imagined.

"I'd better get inside and check on the baby." Samantha hurried to the house. It wouldn't do any good to get too close to her.

"We will leave in the morning."

"Yes, of course you are my guests. I know you won't stay in the house, but what about the barn?"

"Thanks, we can manage."

Patrick nodded and headed toward the cabin. He turned in mid step. "Ya coming, Brian?"

"Yes I am," he yelled as he ran by him. His smile was one of triumph when he reached the door. "I win."

"We are both winners today."

CHAPTER FIVE

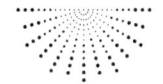

After hating Violet Flower for so long, it felt odd to miss her. They had become something close to friends before she left. What a beautiful baby she'd been blessed with. Envy pinged her heart. Her greatest wish had always been to have a family. The sadness of losing her parents washed over her and it was hard to shake. If only they'd never decided to come west.

She sighed. There was no sense wishing for a different outcome. Dead was dead and she'd have to get over it. They didn't even allow her to take a few of her parent's things with her when they threw her off the wagon train. It was a great loss, deeply felt.

"Are ya okay?" Patrick asked, his eyes full of concern.

"I was just thinking is all. Did you know while you were gone I had decided Violet Flower's name should be Stink Weed?"

He threw his head back and laughed loudly. "Stink Weed?" He laughed some more. "What do ya call me?"

"I haven't had time but I guess I could come up with something." She smiled.

"A good name or bad?" His masculine lips twitched and his eyes sparkled in the firelight.

"Good, I think." They stared at each other until Patrick's smile faded. He grabbed his pipe, put on his coat and was out the door before she could blink. There were times she thought he was attracted to her and then there were times like now, where he would simply up and leave. She'd done it again. She'd made him uncomfortable in his own home.

"Are you going to be my new ma?" Brian asked. He was dutifully practicing his letters in the ashes.

The question startled her. She hadn't thought of it that way.

"Never mind." He sighed and turned his back to her.

"Brian, look at me." She waited for him to turn and his sullen expression pinched her heart. "There are laws about such things. As much as I'd love to be your ma, I doubt a judge would allow it."

"How come?"

"I'm not married and I don't have a way to support either of us."

"You might get married someday, right?"

"I suppose I will but probably not in time for a judge to allow me to be your ma." She knew she cared for the boy but it wasn't until now she realized how much she loved him. The thought of losing him hit her hard.

Brian stared at the floor and shuffled his feet. "I didn't mean to make you sad."

Blinking back tears, she tried to smile. "You didn't. I'm glad we are together now."

"Me too. I'm going out to see Patrick."

"Dress warmly."

He grinned. "I will!"

As soon as the door closed, tears rolled down her face. She dashed them away with the heel of her hand as quickly as she could. There was no sense in getting his hopes up, or hers either. She couldn't imagine how bad his life with Solomon had been. One thing about Brian, he didn't take anything for granted. He just wanted to be loved and to belong.

They both wanted the same thing.

"Why not?" Brian asked Patrick as the door opened. "It's a great idea and I know you like her. You sneak peeks at her when she's not lookin'."

Patrick shook his head in annoyance and his lips formed a grim straight line. He met her gaze and he did not look at all pleased. "Did ya put fool ideas in this boy's head? Ya can't make promises ya can't keep and I never mentioned marrying ya. Sorry but it's not in the plans." He took off his coat, grabbed the bridle he'd been fixing and sat in front of the fire, staring into it.

Her heart plummeted. His opinion of her couldn't be very high if he thought she'd try to get him to marry her. True, she had nowhere to go but she planned to leave come spring. She had hoped she was earning her keep by cooking and cleaning but it was clear she wasn't as welcome as she'd thought. He did genuinely like Brian though. She could see it in the way he looked at him with his big blue eyes. They softened when he talked to the boy.

There was no help for anything now. She'd try to keep out of his way until spring, although it was mighty tough in the small cabin. Having no other outlet for her pent-up frustration, she grabbed a cloth and began to clean.

"Ya know, you've cleaned the same spot five times already." Patrick's voice invaded her thoughts and startled her.

"The cleaner the better." She bit the top of her lip. She needed to stir the stew but Patrick was sitting in her way. Taking a deep breath, she vowed not to fear any man again.

The wooden spoon lay on the counter and she picked it up. She'd have to bend awfully close to Patrick to get near enough to the heavy pot. He might not like her but he liked her cooking. "Excuse me, I need to stir the pot."

"Don't ya think you've stirred things up enough for one day?" He cocked his left brow as he gazed at her.

"I am a decent, God fearing woman. I am very grateful for the roof over my head and for the food to eat. I'm grateful to be warm when it's so cold outside." She decided he wasn't moving so she bent over and as she reached for the pot, her breast touched his knee. He jerked out of her way, sending her flying onto her backside. She blinked a few times before she looked up at him. Her stomach was in knots and her heart felt heavier.

"Why did ya touch me like that?" He sounded offended, angry even.

"It wasn't on purpose. Somehow we've gotten onto the wrong path."

He nodded. "We have. I know better than to become friends with white people. Don't worry, I won't kick ya out." He offered his hand and when she put her small hand in his he pulled her up. He stared into her eyes and she didn't know where else to look. Her hurt finally took over and she turned away.

"Oh, here." She turned back and handed him the spoon. "You need to stir the food."

He stood there unmoving for a moment before he nodded. She wasn't sure what they were both about. Were they even talking to each other? He clearly wouldn't have her here if there were another place for her to stay.

Getting out the ingredients to make biscuits, she wondered about Brian. What had he meant about Patrick peeking at her? She hoped he wasn't trying to get his own way by suggesting marriage. It looked as though he might have picked up some of Solomon's bad ways. She hoped not.

She heard Brian murmuring to Patrick. "I hate it when you fight. I'm going to have to go to an orphanage if you don't stop."

She couldn't hear Patrick's reply, but the loud shuffling of Brian's feet as he made his way to sit on the bed was not a good indication of a happy outcome. There was no rule she and Patrick had to like one another. She just worked for her keep and that was that. It hurt though, everyone always jumped to the wrong conclusion about her. Where was the benefit of the doubt? The people on the wagon train certainly didn't give it to her and now Patrick acted as though she was some hussy. Did she look and act like one?

"I'm hungry."

She gave Brian a smile. "You're always hungry."

He nodded. "True, but I didn't always have food."

He knew how to worm his way into her heart and it wasn't a bad thing. It would hurt when they had to part in the spring, but spring was a ways away.

PATRICK COULDN'T WAIT until the evening meal was over. He'd had all he could take of reining in his temper. Why did women always think marriage was a good thing? It hadn't been good for his mother and no self-respecting white woman would ever allow her breast to brush against him. Just what did she expect from him? Brian he had all figured out. The child was scared and he wanted them to be a family.

It hurt to have to say no, but there would be consequences if he tried to be that boy's father. Dire consequences. He'd learned his lesson long ago not to mix with whites. There was only punishment meted out when he did. The last time nearly killed him. No, he was better off alone and they were safer if they weren't connected to him. The people of the town were a law unto themselves and he didn't wish that on anyone.

He stroked Ahern's neck. "Remember when it was just ya and me? It was good, wasn't it? We liked the quiet and being alone was just fine."

Ahern head butted him. "I know they are growing on me too but they'll be leaving and I don't want to have to suffer the loneliness again. It took me too long to get used to being alone last time." He made sure Ahern was all settled for the night. Maybe they would have an early spring. He hadn't been with a woman in years and it was making him edgy. There was no way he could be attracted to that porcelain doll inside.

He took off his hat, slapped it against his thigh and ran his fingers through his hair. She wasn't a porcelain doll and she'd proven it over and over. He had no call to be upset with her. Truth be told his own desires were turning him into a grizzly. Shaking his head, he winced remembering the hurt in Samantha's eyes, and he'd put it there. Now what? What was he supposed to do now? He wasn't good with people.

He heard her footsteps on the crunchy snow and he didn't turn around.

"Patrick?" Her voice sounded wobbly.

He crumpled his hat with his hand, and then took a deep breath. Slowly he turned with his expression blank. "Did ya want something?"

Her eyes stood out, big and wide on her pale face. "I never, I didn't. Oh darn, what I'm trying to say is I'm not trying to get you to marry me or anything else. If you knew me at all, you'd know better. Perhaps it would be better if I went to live in the cabin where Solomon stayed. Somehow,

I've chased you out of your own house and it's not right. You've been nothing but gracious and I…"

He was a heel and he didn't know how to make things right. "I want ya to stay."

"You have the biggest frown on your face, Patrick. You are not a very good liar. I'll be fine. I know how to chop wood and it should be nice and cozy." She clasped and unclasped her reddened hands.

He strode toward her and took her hands in his. "Ya don't even know to keep your hands warm." The gruffness of his voice surprised him.

"I can't stay, Patrick. Your opinion of me is unbearable. I don't think I can stand to look at you every day. I'm sure you feel the same about me."

He rubbed her hands with his. There was something between them. He felt it every time she was near. He wanted to kiss away her sorrow but he didn't dare. Dropping her hands, he gave her a sad smile. "We'll have to put up with each other until spring. Winter in these mountains has claimed too many lives." His heart dropped as she blinked a few times before she gave him a curt nod. She pulled her hands away and took a giant step back, away from him.

"You're right. These mountains are harsh. I was just trying to make it easier for you and I agree we can put up with each other. Good night." There were tears forming as she turned from him.

"*Damn!*" His heart cried out for him to stop her and pull her into his arms but his head knew better. "Damn," he whispered into the night.

He waited until the lamp in the house turned down before he went inside. A sigh of relief passed over his chilled lips. They were both in bed, and he wouldn't have to talk to either of them. He got his bed in front of the fire ready and lay down. Life wasn't fair and he'd learned over and over again just how unfair it could be but it never hurt this much before. Nothing felt right, especially his bed. The floor felt harder than usual and he could hear Samantha tossing and turning. It was his fault she wasn't sleeping. Finally, he couldn't take it anymore and he got up and went to the side of the bed. "Do ya want to talk?"

Most of her hair had escaped from her usual braid and stood in all directions. "Yes." She quickly and quietly got out of bed and joined him in front of the fireplace.

"I haven't been very nice to ya lately and I'm sorry. I told ya a little about my childhood but I didn't tell ya about Maeve." He stood up and started making tea. Once he had it on the fire, he sat back down. "We started out as fishing buddies. Her parents didn't care where she was as long as she didn't bother them. Her father couldn't keep a job and it wasn't a happy place for her. We understood each other. We were the children the other parents didn't want their children to play with." He paused as happy memories of her replaced the hate in his heart.

"We grew into young adults and planned to be married. I really should have known better but I was too foolish to think of the consequences. I guess it was fine as long as we were street urchins, but our friendship wasn't approved of when we grew into adults. I did know there would be a few busybodies who might stand in our way. After all we lived in their town."

Samantha laid her hand on his arm and it warmed him. He was afraid he'd see pity but he saw understanding instead.

"There was a barn dance and I asked her to go with me. She thought it a bad idea but I wanted to stand up for us. I wanted the same respect everyone got. We didn't have good clothes to wear, but I picked flowers for her hair. She had chestnut hair and green eyes. Her eyes sparkled in excitement as I escorted her toward the dance. At first people didn't notice us and I was fine with it. Maeve began to grow apprehensive and she wanted to leave. I guess she felt the shifting of the crowd's mood. I dragged her onto the dance floor and we were instantly grabbed, both from behind."

He took a long sip of his coffee and shook his head. "I was taken out back and beat half to death. Maeve, well Maeve refused to tell me what happened to her, but she had bruises on her I wouldn't wish on my worst enemy. I could hardly walk but I made it to her house. Not only did she refrain from talking about it, she told me to go away and never come back. I told her she'd feel differently in a day or two but she said she could no longer be associated with a 'dirty Indian'."

"Oh, Patrick." She squeezed his arm and he gently covered her hand with his.

"There was nothing for me in town any longer. I swallowed my pride and tried to see Maeve a couple more times but she refused to see me. I didn't have money or a horse. I took my clothes and rifle and lit out. It was fall and I like ya ended up lost in the snow."

"You're here now." Her gentle voice soothed him.

"Yes thanks to a trapper named Otter. He found me same as I found ya. I wintered with him and he taught me everything I needed to know to survive. We trapped together for a year then he told me I had made enough on the pelts, I needed to make my own way."

"How long ago was that?"

"I've been on my own for about ten years now."

"And I'm an intrusion. I do appreciate all you've done for me. I'm not sure how to act around you. I'm a woman of good moral character and if I did or said… I don't know. Is it the way I look? Is there something about me that has people believing the worst? The women on the wagon train thought I'd try to entice their husbands and you—well you think I'm trying to tempt you. Violet Flower saw the same flaw in me and for the love of God I don't know what I'm doing wrong." Her eyes grew wide as she stared into his, as though searching for an answer. He did this, he'd made her distraught.

"I don't know about the wagon train except maybe you're too pretty. Same with Violet Flower, she seemed to think of ya as competition."

She took her hand off his arm and wrapped her arms around her middle. "And you? I'm not buying the pretty thing. I'm plain and I know it. But even if they thought I was pretty, it doesn't explain your actions." Her voice grew hoarse as she dropped her gaze to the floor.

"Ya are pretty, beautiful actually, and the fact ya don't know it is endearing. Ya are a hard worker, ya roll with the hardest punches and ya have a big heart. I have the problem. Don't ya see? I refuse to go near another white woman again. It's not allowed. There is no way a judge would allow me to raise Brian. I'd only cause ya pain and misery and it would hurt too much when ya left." He closed his eyes, leaned his elbows on his knees and put his face in his hands.

"So, you don't really hate me?"

"No, sweetheart, I don't, but I'm not going to love ya either." Something broke inside him as he said the words. It was final.

"I'll just let you go to sleep, Patrick. I understand, really I do and I wouldn't want to be the cause of your pain."

He watched as she padded across the room and got into bed. He knew he should do the same but he wouldn't sleep. He was mourning the death of dreams. Somehow, he thought he was done with such feelings but here they were stabbing his heart in the worst possible way.

He finally lay in front of the fire watching the multicolored flames, enjoying the cracking and popping of the wood. Eventually, he fell asleep.

THE NEXT MORNING Samantha finished washing up the breakfast dishes. While it was a relief to know it wasn't something she did, she took no comfort in it. Patrick's sad story pained her, and his actions were understandable. She grabbed a cloth and carefully lifted the coffee from the fire.

"I still don't know why I can't drink coffee. I'm practically a man." Brian wore his mulish expression.

"I have tea made too. It's not good for a young person to drink coffee."

"How would you know? I used to drink it all the time and I think I should know what's good for me and what's not." He crossed his arms over his chest and jutted out his bottom lip.

"I'm the adult and I know what's best."

"Sure you know. You were the one who got thrown off a wagon train and went traipsing through the woods. You were a meal for bears. Besides, you can't tell me what to do. I'm going to stay here and live with Patrick. You'll be leaving soon enough."

A slap to the face would have felt better than his disrespect. Somehow, she'd thought they'd formed a bond together. She was wrong.

"From the look of the sky I doubt anyone will be going anywhere soon." Patrick came inside with two buckets filled with snow.

Her face heated. He must have heard their conversation. She grabbed one of her stockings, sat in a chair and began to look for all the holes. Violet Flower had fashioned a needle out of a piece of bone and she hoped to mend the garment.

"She won't let me have coffee. I've had enough of being treated like a child. I've done a man's work for a few years now." Brian gave her a sour look, and then stared at Patrick, probably waiting for him to agree.

Patrick put the buckets by the fire and sat in the other chair. "All three of us come from different backgrounds. I grew up dirt poor, ya were made to grow up too fast and Samantha here probably knows what's right and wrong better than we do. Yelling at her isn't going to help."

"So I can have coffee?"

"I'll have to talk it over with Samantha. It wouldn't do to go against her wishes if she has good reason."

"I don't understand why she gets a say anyway. I'm staying with ya. I'm not going to live in town with that woman."

Her eyes grew wide and her heart pained her. "You're right Brian, I can't make you do anything. I'm not your ma or guardian. I thought we were at least friends but I have a lot to learn."

"Like you snore like a horse all night long."

"Brian, that's enough."

"But she does." Brian smiled.

Without a word, she stood, bundled up and went outside. She bit the inside of her cheek to keep from crying. How she wished her parents had never tried to go west. She scanned the sky and frowned at the plethora of dark clouds. Patrick was right. They were in for a storm. The wind began to pick up. She quickly used the necessary and went into the barn. It was too soon to go into the house.

A lone tear trailed down her face. All she wanted was a place to call home, surrounded by people who cared for her. Brian's true feelings were a surprising blow. Had the closeness and love she felt between them all been a farce? It was just as well he planned to stay with Patrick.

She laid a horse blanket on a bale of hay and curled up on it. She could roll with the punches. Patrick didn't know what he was talking about. She wasn't the type to take things in stride. Life wasn't easy for her. She wished she could just tell herself Brian didn't mean what he said but there was a gleam in his eye and he meant to hurt her.

She heard the crunch of snow under his feet and she quickly stood. Patrick was a good-looking man and she wished things could be different between them. "I'm going back in. You didn't have to come get me." Her voice was low and soft.

"I figured ya were probably getting cold out here."

Swallowing hard, she nodded, staring at her feet. If she looked up, he'd know she'd been crying and she was certain she wasn't done. "I'm fine. Go on in and I'll follow in a bit."

Patrick put his finger under her chin and lifted it until they stared into each other's eyes. She must have looked bad because he winced. He cupped her cheek in his calloused hand and stroked her cheekbone with his thumb.

"Brian is just a child. He didn't mean what he said."

Tears started to fall. "He meant it. I thought we were close, but the truth of it is he wants to have his own way or he pushes me away. There is no hesitation or regret in his eyes ever. It's my fault really. I let him into my heart and now it feels shattered."

"He doesn't know what he wants. He's not used to a kind-hearted woman like ya. He has natural defenses to keep himself from getting too hurt. It was probably the only way he survived being with Solomon." He wiped her tears with the pad of his thumb.

"Sometimes I feel so alone and empty and it scares me. I have no family, I have no one. I'll survive, I'm not worried about that. It's the uncertainty of my future, the loss of my parents and I thought Brian had bonded with me. It was probably just dreaming on my part. I suppose I'm a bit touched in the head. God has forgotten about me and I'm scared."

"From what I know of God, he never forgets, he just

answers in his own time." He smiled. "Don't look so surprised. My father was a good Catholic and he made sure I knew the word of God. I resented it at the time but believing in God is what I hold onto when I don't think I can go on."

He certainly was a complicated man. She really didn't know much about him at all. He believed in God and she hadn't known it. He was a good man and it was enough. His closeness made her heart pound and she wished with everything in her it would stop. The fact she loved him made her feel emptier. Patrick would not love her back. "Thank you for coming out here." She gently lifted his hands off her face and stepped back. "You're right, it is cold." She walked around him and out of the barn. What she needed to do was get herself together. There was nowhere to hide her feelings and she didn't want their pity. He was right behind her. She could feel the warmth of his body as she hesitated to open the door.

"It's all going to be okay," he reassured her.

He was right, she'd overreacted. She opened the door and went into the warm snug cabin. She had a lot to think about and keeping her emotions to herself would probably occupy her time. It was going to be torture living with the two males, knowing she loved them but they didn't love her back. She walked to the bed, sat down, bowed her head and prayed.

CHAPTER SIX

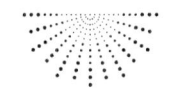

Patrick wished he didn't know how much Samantha cared about him. She tried to avoid any touching, in depth conversations, or lingering glances. He never would have imagined how much it hurt. The last few weeks he'd had to remind himself it was for the best, time after time. The urge to crush her to him and take the sadness away from her grew daily.

Brian didn't seem too affected by Samantha's withdrawal. He didn't even seem to notice. He was a good child who'd had a hard life. Patrick didn't think he meant to hurt her. He helped around the place and continued his reading. Samantha was very stiff around him. The natural affection she'd had disappeared.

Sitting in front of the big fireplace repairing a frayed bridle, he felt her gaze on him. He wasn't sure if he should look at her or not. Figuring he had nothing to lose, he lifted his gaze to hers. He arched his eyebrow at her continued stare.

"Do you happen to know the date? I'm afraid I've lost track."

"It's December as near as I can tell."

"What about Christmas?"

"What about it?"

"I'm wondering if we missed it."

He shrugged his shoulders. "Makes no difference to me and I doubt Brian has ever celebrated it."

She gave him a sad smile and a curt nod before she turned from him.

He could make up a date to make her happy but somehow it seemed wrong. "I'll go hunting tomorrow and see what I can find. We can have a big dinner if it would make ya happy."

She stilled for a long time and he wondered what she was thinking. Finally she turned. "Thank you. It really doesn't matter what day we celebrate. We do have a bit of sugar I could make sugar candy." Her eyes brightened and her cheeks turned pink.

His heart jumped and he inwardly cursed. He couldn't find an even keel with the woman. He was either ignoring her or mooning over her like an ignorant boy. He almost groaned aloud. She looked happy and somehow her happiness linked to his. At least he'd be gone a lot of the day tomorrow hunting. Maybe a bit of fresh air could help him keep his mind off her soft pink lips. "Sugar candy sounds nice. I can't remember the last time I had candy."

"It'll make the day special." She held his gaze until he couldn't stand looking and not touching.

"What do you think, Brian?"

"I've never had candy. It's real good ain't it?" He smiled at Samantha and she smiled back. At least they were getting along better. "Ain't you going to say ain't ain't a word?"

She threw the piece of cloth she'd been holding at him and he flinched. His face turned red as he bent to retrieve the towel and he handed it back to her.

"Brian, no one is going to hurt you again, least of all me." Her voice was sweet and soft.

"You won't mean to, but you will. One day you'll leave me behind somewhere. Maybe here, maybe the orphanage. You'll be sad but grownups always do what is best. They make promises and break them."

There was a lot of truth in Brian's words but Patrick didn't know what to say. More than likely Brian would be left in an orphanage, leaving them broken hearted. He wished he had some pull, or respect even, in town, but he was an outcast. His heart ached. Keeping them warm, dry and fed was the best he could do.

"We don't need to talk about it now," Samantha said. She smiled but it didn't reach her eyes. "We're going to have Christmas tomorrow. I'm looking forward to it."

Brian scoffed. "I suppose Santa will be arriving tonight."

Her brow furrowed as though she hadn't thought about presents. "Maybe—"

"Save it. I know he doesn't exist, at least not for children like me." He plopped down on a chair and frowned.

Patrick didn't know what to say but Samantha's pleading gaze got to him. "No, Brian, ya are good. Ya do a man's work without complaint. It's just, well I don't know. Santa Claus never came to leave me presents either. I did hear tell he has a time of it trying to get to the children in the west. I'm looking forward to the candy. It'll be a big treat for me."

He must have got it right because Samantha bestowed a beautiful smile on him.

"The reason for Christmas isn't only presents. It's the celebration of the birth of Jesus. I don't know if you know much about him—"

"I don't want to hear about him."

"That's fine. Maybe one day you will."

Patrick raised his eyebrows. Most times people tried to

jam their religion down his throat. There were many times helpful citizens thought heathens just needed saving. Little did they know his father was a very religious man. Samantha's answer was a breath of fresh air and it warmed him.

He hadn't realized he was staring at her until she blushed a deep red. He quickly turned away. Tomorrow couldn't come soon enough. He'd spend the morning outside alone.

Rustling noises disturbed Samantha's sleep and relief swept through her when she found it was Patrick getting something from under the bed. It probably was some hunting thing. Turning over, she went back to sleep.

The next time she woke, it was morning. She got up, dressed quickly, and rebraided her hair. Next, she inched around Patrick and put a pot of melted snow on the fire to warm. His eyes opened and he smiled. Why did he have to look so ruggedly handsome?

"Good morning. Did ya sleep well?" he asked as he sat up and stretched. His magnificent chest came into view and she couldn't take her eyes off him.

"I don't know. I think we might have mice."

His smile faded. "Why do ya think that?"

"I heard rustling under the bed last night." She couldn't help the small laugh that bubbled up.

He nodded. "Ah, yes I believe I heard it too." He grabbed more logs and put them on the fire.

"Did Santa come?" The wistfulness in Brian's voice hurt. Perhaps she shouldn't have mentioned Christmas at all.

"I'm sorry."

"As a matter of fact, I see something on the table. Why don't you see what it is?" Patrick's nod reassured her.

Brian flew out of bed and ran to the table. "Oh boy! Sam, come look."

She flashed Patrick a grateful smile and went to Brian's side. "A knife?"

"Yes, and look it has a leather sheath and everything. Santa didn't forget me after all." Brian's exuberance filled the house.

"This is wonderful." She wanted to ask who on earth gives a child a knife but she couldn't bring herself to spoil Brian's fun.

Patrick pulled a chair out and sat at the table. "Show me."

Brian excitedly displayed his new treasure. They talked about using the knife and how to be careful. Brian seemed to know many of the things Patrick was explaining. Maybe the knife wasn't such a bad idea at all. She went about her morning routine of making tea and breakfast and before she knew it, Patrick was out the door. His eagerness to be away seemed to grow each day.

It was understandable and she tried to tell herself it was for the best but there were times when it battered her heart. It struck her it was her first Christmas without her parents and tears threatened. Taking a deep breath, she turned and smiled at Brian. "Let's get to the candy."

"Oh, boy!"

It was such an easy thing to do, but sugar was too dear to make candy any other time. She placed the big pot over the fire and added snow and when it heated, she added the sugar. "Here Brian take this pan and pack it with clean snow. I'll pour the sugar over it and it will harden into candy." She barely had the last word out before he went flying out the door.

Arctic air hit her and she shook her head. Brian forgot to close the door but he reappeared before she had a chance to get up. "Is this enough?"

It was amazing the difference a little excitement made. There was no brooding, or casts of doubt today. "It certainly is. Set it on the table and I'll pour this into ribbons. It will harden and turn into candy."

"When will it be ready?"

She laughed. "Probably right before Patrick gets back."

"We don't know when he'll be back."

"Same for the candy, you just have to let it set."

Brian sat, grabbed a stick and started to whittle it with his knife as Patrick had done several times. She watched intently, her stomach drawn tight, waiting for him to cut himself. After a time she relaxed. He seemed to know what he was doing.

They spent the morning in a happy quiet, waiting for Patrick and waiting for the candy.

A couple hours later, they quickly broke up the long ribbons and she waited for Brian to pop a piece into his mouth. When he did, she realized his happiness was her happiness. Sheer joy crossed his face and he gave her the biggest smile ever.

"I take it you like it."

"I sure do! Maybe this Christmas stuff is a good idea."

The door opened and Patrick came in, handed her venison wrapped in cloth and mussed Brian's hair with his hand. The gesture was so natural she had to glance away. She might mean well, but Brian was right. She couldn't promise to keep him when she doubted it would actually happen.

"Hey no frowns, it's Christmas," Patrick chided.

"I know, just missing my folks I guess."

He took her hand into his. There was such a contrast in size and strength. "It's a hard thing, losing the ones ya love. I know it's still fresh for ya." His eyes softened.

"Thank you, your understanding helps. Well, I'd better get

the meal started." She pulled her hand from his, wishing she could have prolonged the contact.

"Patrick! Try the candy. You will love it." Brian picked up a piece and handed it to Patrick. He watched intently as Patrick put it in his mouth and closed his eyes. "Great, isn't it? Guess what? I helped."

Patrick chuckled. "Ya did a fine job."

Brian beamed at the praise. "I've been whittling too, just like you."

"It seems I missed all the fun."

"No, we can whittle together now." Brian's exuberance lifted her spirits. She was safe and with people she cared about.

Dinner was a surprisingly relaxing affair. Was just being here the reason? Conversation, smiles and glances that didn't have hidden meanings relieved her. Today she didn't worry so much about pauses, silences or if she was giving out some mysterious signals. She was free game. This whole time she'd been worried about her feelings but they didn't matter. Patrick wasn't kissing her anymore. In fact, he'd been a bit distant at times. Her imagination got the better of her at times but they were her worries, not his. As for Brian, this might be all the time she'd have with him. She'd make the best of it and try not to dread saying good-bye.

"What a fine Christmas." She smiled at them both. "I can't remember a nicer one. Thank you both." She'd never forget the smile on Brian's face or his bright eyes of surprise when he spotted the knife.

CHAPTER SEVEN

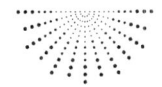

"It's past the point of hurt, Ahern," Patrick said as he brushed down his horse. "It'll be just as bad if not worse than before. I think it might take a bit longer this time to get used to being alone."

He grabbed the lead rope and started walking toward his first trap. It had been two weeks since their celebration and it had been hell. He wanted Samantha with a ferocity he had a hard time managing. He'd invented more reasons to be outside. He finally didn't give a reason, he just left. She was too close, too pretty, and too appealing. Each time she smiled he felt gut kicked. It was torture.

"I'm glad it warmed up a might, old boy. I know, I know you've been in the barn way too long. Still we have to be careful." He was used to talking to Ahern. He was a good listener.

He heard a wail and stopped. He listened again, trying to figure out what animal it could be. He ripped off his snowshoes and sprang up onto Ahern's back. "Sounds like Samantha." Ahern must have sensed his urgency. Patrick kept reining him in, not wanting him injured by the slushy cold snow.

It only took a few minutes but it seemed longer. What could have happened? He shook his head. Anything could happen out here. The cabin door stood open and Patrick grabbed his rifle, jumped down off the horse's back and ran into the cabin, ready to shoot.

"What happened?"

"I need your help. Brian cut himself and it's so deep I can't get the bleeding to stop." Her hands shook as she grabbed Brian's right hand and showed his sliced palm.

He took off his outerwear and pulled a chair up next to Brian's. "Let me see." It was deep, very deep. "I need water."

"I already tried—"

"Just do it. I need to know we tried everything before I turn to using heat."

She turned white. "Like Violet Flower's wound?"

Their gazes met and he nodded. Immediately fresh water was at his side with wet, wrung out pieces of cloth. He cleaned the blood away and pressed a cloth into the palm.

"It hurts." Brian's color had drained from his face.

"I know, son, I know. Do the best ya can. Scream out if it helps."

Brian nodded and bit his bottom lip.

The bleeding didn't stop. "Grab my whiskey it—"

"Solomon drank it all."

"Sit, before ya faint."

Samantha promptly sat on one of the crates. "I could try to sew it."

"Not with the needle ya have. It'll tear his skin to pieces. Damn, I should have the right supplies. My needle broke the last time I stitched myself up and I didn't replace it." He took his big buck knife and placed it into the hot coals. It would hurt like hell, but it was the only option. He'd had to do it to himself a time or two but a young boy was different.

"Samantha, do ya think ya could get a bucket of clean snow? It'll be best to have for after."

"After what?" Brian's voice quavered and his eyes grew wide.

"After we fix ya up."

He snatched his hand back from Patrick. "You ain't cuttin' my hand off."

"Nothing drastic, I promise."

They waited for Samantha to return. She put the bucket right next to Brian. If only he could take her worry away, but he was worried too. He took Brian's hand in his and without preamble, took the hot knife and pressed it against the wound. The searing sound and the smell of burnt flesh nauseated him and he didn't dare look at Samantha. She was still sitting, a good sign.

Brian's scream echoed through the cabin and continued long after his hand was in the bucket of snow.

Patrick grabbed a bandage out of his bag and placed it over Brian's wound. Then he lifted the boy out of the chair and carried him to the bed. Samantha hurried over to pull the covers down. "He's passed out."

Samantha nodded. "It's for the best."

Grabbing her hand, he led her to the chairs and they sat down. "Tell me, what happened. Was he whittling?" Guilt bubbled up inside of him.

"No, no. Don't blame yourself. It was my fault. I should have been watching but I went outside to use the necessary and I had meat and a knife out. I planned to cut it up for supper and he decided to help. I came back into his cry and all that blood. I think I screamed."

"I heard ya. He should be fine now and don't blame yourself. Children get hurt all the time, especially boys."

"Still, I just don't think."

He stood up and pulled her up in front of him. "Ya think too much."

She opened her mouth to reply and he swooped down and kissed her sweet lips. She moaned as the kiss deepened and he pulled her closer until their bodies touched. His hell had turned into heaven. The sensation of her fingers running through his hair made his nerves come alive. Her nipples hardened against his chest and he almost surrendered to her sweetness. Slowly he pulled away. "I'm—"

Reaching up, she placed her fingers over his lips. "I'm not. I think comforting each other is only natural after what happened. I was so afraid and thank the Lord you came when you did. I'm grateful." She stared into his eyes and he tried not to flinch at the word 'grateful'. It wasn't a kiss of gratitude for him.

"We'll have to watch him and make sure the flesh searing worked." He stepped away from her. "He's a good child ."

Her hands busily patted her hair into place. "Yes, yes he is."

Damn, he couldn't think of one single reason to go outside. Instead, he grabbed the snowshoes he was fashioning for Samantha, pulled a chair closer to the fire and worked away. Try as he might he couldn't concentrate and he spent the afternoon watching her clean the blood up, then the bloody rags, which she hung to dry before she began to make supper. Maybe he should have offered to cook. She probably would have said no. She was doing her darndest to stay busy.

A CRY in the dark of night woke her and she sat straight up. Next to her Brian was thrashing all around. She put her hand on his skin and panicked at its heat. She jumped out of bed and Patrick immediately came to her side.

"Fever?" he asked.

"I'm afraid so."

Patrick reached over and laid his hand on Brian's forehead. "It's a bad one. I'll run out and get more snow."

Numbly she nodded. People often died of fever. The end usually started with a fever. How many people from the wagon train had she tried to nurse due to a fever? Closing her eyes, she took a deep breath and lit the lamp. She grabbed a few of the dried clothes and brought a chair right next to the bed. There was no time for anything but concentrating on Brian. Not everyone died, she reminded herself.

She nodded her thanks as Patrick put the snow into a basin and handed it to her. Gently she set the basin on the chair and crawled into bed, next to Brian. As she wet the cloth with the frigid snow, she said a silent prayer for healing.

"We can take turns."

"What?" She'd forgotten Patrick stood next to her.

"We can take turns tending to Brian." Worry lined his face.

"Sure. He'll be fine."

Patrick gave her shoulder a quick squeeze.

Hours later, exhaustion hit her. Brian had been crying out, "Don't beat me," over and over, and it hurt her soul. Patrick tried to get her to lie on his makeshift bed in front of the fire, but she refused. Brian needed her.

"Sometimes it gets worse before it gets better," Patrick told her as he swallowed hard.

"Yes, it does."

"I'm sure he'll be fine."

She nodded. The look of doubt on Patrick's face proved them both liars. Her heart twisted as she continued to bathe him with cold water. There was no way to tell if the wound had become infected. The whole section was fiery red-burnt flesh. She shouldn't have left the knife out. She should have told him not to touch it. Maybe they shouldn't have praised him for doing the work of a man.

The bed dipped beside her as Patrick sat down. He gently took the cloth from her and put it on the chair. "He's drenched." He placed his strong arms around her and pulled her back against him, cradling her with his body.

Her chin wobbled and she bit her bottom lip to stem her tears, but they refused to stop. Patrick tightened his hold, kissed the side of her neck and rocked back and forth. His comfort filled her. She wasn't alone. For so long now she'd felt alone and a bit afraid. Especially where her future was concerned. Patrick planned to take them to town in the spring, and then what? Right now only one thing mattered; getting Brian well.

"If he's not better by morning, I'll rig up the travois and take him to town. There's a doctor there."

"The weather isn't good and it will take days."

"We'll talk about it in the morning. We have enough worries now. The poor child has been through so much and all he wanted was a family."

She waited for him to continue, to say they were or would be a family, but no such declaration came. He may care for her but not enough to go against the town. She didn't want to meet people who could be so cruel to a person but for Brian's sake, she'd go. She laid her hands over his, marveling at the difference in size. He was a big strong mountain man but he was also a gentle soul. He probably didn't relish taking them to town, but he would because he was a good man. Her eyes began to close.

"Sleep, tomorrow will be hard trekking through the snow."

She slept much longer than intended. Patrick shook her shoulder gently and told her it was time. Her eyes flew open and her breath hitched in her chest until she saw Brian breathing. Slowly her breathing returned. "What do you need me to do?"

"I need ya to gather the dried venison and some of the canned goods. Ya and I will have to walk while Ahern pulls the travois. I'll wrap your feet in fur before we put your snowshoes on."

"Should I bathe his face again?"

"No, it'll be cold enough as it is on the way."

"You're worried."

"I am. I'm hoping the weather holds and we all make it to town alive. If ya want to stay—"

"Never, I'm going. Give me a few minutes to get ready." She touched Brian's face and winced. His fever hadn't broken. She'd helped to nurse enough people to know his illness would more than likely end with death.

Jumping out of bed, she got everything ready while Patrick hitched the travois to Ahern. The days were shorter in the winter and they needed to leave right away. She wrapped her feet in the furs he left by her snowshoes and then strapped the shoes on. Standing, she almost fell forward. They would take some getting used to.

The door swung open and Patrick nodded his approval as he came through it. He lifted her and carried her out to the snow. "The stairs." He went back in without another word. He was right, she'd have fallen head first if she had tried to step down.

He brought out the supplies and tied the packs to Ahern. Lastly he carried Brian wrapped in furs out of the cabin and gently laid him onto the travois. "I'll lead the horse and you can trail after. It'll be easier walking for you."

The wind whipped around them, carrying her words with

them. It would be treacherous but it was something they had to do. Brian looked almost dead under all the furs. He hadn't moved but maybe he was getting more rest without all the thrashing and crying out. Swallowing hard, she took one step then another in her snowshoes. They were a bit cumbersome but she had better balance and her fear of falling lessened with each step.

Patrick noted the position of the sun in the blue sky. It was time to find a place to camp. There was a cave another mile or so up the trail, but he wasn't sure Samantha could make it. She was a strong woman, no doubt about it. He knew men who would have asked for breaks long before. He offered to put her on Ahern's back for a bit but she refused.

Brian woke a few times and they gave him water, but he didn't know where he was. He didn't recognize him or Samantha. He wished he could take the worry from Samantha, but it wasn't in his power.

At least it hadn't snowed, but the wind made the world frigid. His hands and feet were feeling it. He kept walking with his head down, into the wind. He only hoped there would be help for Brian when they got to town. If they kept up this pace tomorrow, they'd shave almost a day off their travels.

He'd only had to travel this far in the winter once when someone broke into his cabin and stole his rations. He'd been tempted to go to Otter for help, but he was a grown man who could do for himself. He'd made it then, and they'd make it now.

He slowed the procession to a halt and looked back. Samantha's face was bright red and her movements were slowing. "We'll set up camp," he yelled.

She merely nodded and waited for him to start moving again.

Ahern seemed just as glad to be stopping too. He saw the cave and made his way right to it. *Smart horse*. They'd been there before, but still Ahern was special. Patrick unhitched the travois, grabbed up Brian and carried him into the cave. It was cold but the wood he left there from his last trip lay on the ground. They'd have a fire tonight. Some of the tension left his body as he lay Brian down. He went back out and grabbed Samantha's hand. "Come, I'll get a fire going in a bit." She followed stiffly and he knew she was going to be in a world of hurt before long.

"It's a relief to be out of the wind," she said as her teeth chattered.

"I need to tend to Ahern, and then I'll be in." He didn't wait for an answer. Ahern first, without him they'd be stuck, then a fire, then do it all again tomorrow.

His eyes widened when he entered the cave. A nice fire was blazing and Samantha was trying to get Brian to drink some water. Her body shook and she winced when she moved. His admiration for her grew. He'd never known a woman her equal. She was kind and giving and thought of others first.

After removing his snowshoes, he grabbed the coffee pot, filled it with the snow right outside the cave and put it on to heat. He rummaged through a bag until he found the tea. He smiled. Brian was allowed to drink tea. He still didn't understand why he wasn't supposed to drink coffee but there was a heap of things he didn't know.

Samantha turned and moved until she sat as near the fire as possible. "I can hardly feel my hands and feet."

"I know. Just sit there and thaw. We'll unwrap your coverings slowly so it won't be too painful."

"Will it hurt like last time?"

"No, last time ya were out in the cold for days without the proper wear. You'll be just fine."

Her stare was full of doubt, but she nodded. "Brian's fever is the same and I looked at his hand. It's still bright red from the cauterizing so I don't know if it's infected."

He nodded. "I'll get ya there tomorrow."

"How? You said two to three days."

"Take the covering off your hands."

"Oh! They don't hurt and I can feel them." She smiled brightly. The light of the fire bathed her in colors of yellow and orange.

"I do know a thing or two." He chuckled softly.

"Now how can we get there so fast?"

"I put ya on Ahern and ya and Brian ride to town. You'll be there before sundown."

Her brow furrowed as she bit her lip. "Alone? I don't think it's a good idea. I mean, we could get lost or there are animals out there."

Nodding, he tried to give her a smile of reassurance. "I know it's scary but it may be Brian's only chance. I want to do whatever it takes for the boy. I'll be trailing behind and if ya go off the path, I'll find ya."

"I still don't think we should split up. Maybe we could both ride the horse."

"He's a strong horse but he won't make it to town with my added weight. He's pulling Brian too."

The fire was the focus of her stare. She said nothing for a long time while he made the tea, grabbed leftover biscuits, and dried venison. "We should think on this."

"We don't have the time."

Brian cried out in his sleep and Samantha went to soothe him. He hoped she'd agree it was probably Brian's only hope.

"I'll do it. I'm afraid, but I'll do it. You promise to meet us in town?" Her stare grew intense.

"Of course I will." He sounded more optimistic than he felt. Her body visibly relaxed at his words. He hated the damn town and its residents. Samantha would see what they thought of him, how they treated him. She'd never look his way again. His heart squeezed. It would have happened eventually but he loved her.

She pulled the furs up around Brian, then came to the fire, and sat next to him. Taking his hand, she squeezed it. "I realize we've been a burden to you and I thank you for all you've done. You kept us safe this whole time. I hope the sun shines bright tomorrow."

"Aye, I hope so too." He gazed into her eyes. Her feelings for him showed on her face and it tore at him. Those feelings would soon change. He leaned toward her and she tilted her head back giving him access to her lush lips. His groan echoed in the cave. The kiss was so sweet, so full of emotion and when she opened her mouth to him, he knew he was a goner. She reached up and pulled his head down to kiss him harder, deeper.

He lifted her until she sat on his lap, straddling him. The way she shivered when he trailed kisses down her neck drove him wild. He took her mouth again, and then pulled her close in a tight hug.

"I finally feel warm," she murmured.

"Me too." He never wanted to let her go. She was his but only for the moment. The need for her grew until his body's response was very uncomfortable, still he held her. It was worth the ache to have her in his arms. It was both a hello, and a goodbye. She loved him, he was certain yet it wouldn't be. He'd make sure she got to town and all settled before he left. There was no reason for her to come back with him. The townspeople probably wouldn't allow it anyway.

There were too many furs between them but he didn't dare hold her any closer. Her fingers ran through his hair as he stroked her back. His heart clenched. She was the light, the tenderness, the joy he'd missed in his life. Why couldn't he just live in the moment instead of already experiencing the heartache of parting?

Patrick gently lay Brian on the travois and covered him. He leaned over and kissed the boy's head. Samantha's chest hurt and tears pricked at the back of her eyes. If only they could all go together, but Patrick was right. She needed to get Brian to town quickly. Patrick approached and she bit her bottom lip to keep from telling him of her love for him. He didn't want her love.

"Head East along the trail. Let Ahern pick his pace. He'll go as fast as possible and as safe as possible. When ya get to town head to the second set of buildings on the left. Doc Hanks will help ya. If there is no answer, go to the general store across the street. Mrs. Andrews, a widow lady, will help."

Staring into his blue eyes, she tried to remember everything he said. He didn't say it but she knew this was goodbye. Oh, she'd see him, but it was goodbye to what could have been between them. He was already building a wall between them.

"Patrick, I—"

He put his hands on her hips, kissed her cheek and set her on Ahern. She didn't get a chance to hold him close. "It's best ya get going. I'll be about three hours behind by the time ya get to town. You'll be fine. The rifle is in the scabbard if ya need it."

Nodding she put on her best smile. "I'll see you tonight."

"Tonight." He stepped back and gave Ahern a light slap on the rump. Off they went.

The urge to cry overwhelmed her but she willed her tears away, simply because she was afraid, they'd freeze on her face. The wind whipped and chapped her cheeks as they headed into town. For a time she could look back and catch sight of Patrick but eventually, he was too far behind. All was quiet except for the wind rushing through the trees. It was both lovely and eerie at the same time.

Brian was her main concern and she chastised herself for being selfish. She didn't matter, Patrick didn't matter, it was Brian who mattered. His life was considerably more important than her tender heart. She kept flexing her fingers and toes so they didn't get too stiff.

The cry of a bobcat caught her off guard and she reached for the rifle, placing it across her lap. Ahern just kept on and although she looked, she didn't catch sight of the animal. She hoped Patrick was doing fine. What if the bobcat…

They shouldn't have split up. She had the rifle. No, he had one too. The cold seemed to be affecting her thinking. Thankfully, the trail was easy to stay on. It was a big swath of bare land in the midst of a sea of trees. The sky appeared angry. Dark clouds rolled in and all she could do was hope and pray the bad weather would hold off.

Chilled to the bone, she hunched over, trying to stay warm. Her whole body screamed at her to stop but if she got off, she knew she wouldn't have the strength to get herself back on Ahern. Finally, just as the sun began to fade, the forest gave way to a town. Funny, she never asked the name of the town and the sign was covered over with snow.

It took forever to get to the town. She passed the first set of buildings and stopped at the second looking for the doctor. After a minute, she spotted the sign and slid down the side of Ahern, holding on to him the whole time. Her legs were too frozen to hold her up so she leaned into his side, taking a deep breath.

Thankfully, she was soon surrounded by people who wanted to help. One man lifted Brian and carried him into the doctor's office while two women helped her to follow right behind. "The horse—"

"He'll be at the livery, Ma'am. I'll take good care of him." She only heard the man. She couldn't turn to see him. She nodded and continued on, thankful for the help.

"Brian."

"The doc is looking at him," the taller woman said.

"Here, let's get you out of these wet clothes and warmed up," said the other woman.

They led her into what appeared to be the doctor's living quarters and sat her down in front of a wood burning stove. Soon she was sitting there in her dress with a blanket over her. "I need to be with Brian."

"The doctor is taking care of your son. He'll be here in a minute to let you know. Meanwhile I'm Mary Agnes Breeze, dear, are you alright? Are you hurt in any way?" Samantha started to shake her head at the kindly older woman. Her blue eyes held compassion.

"What she means is why are you on that horse? You haven't been attacked, have you? I know who owns that particular horse and I think it best if the doctor examines you. How did you get away?" The taller woman's voice grated. Her dark eyes flashed as she kept patting her dark hair.

"Get away?" Her brow furrowed as she tried to understand what the woman was talking about.

"Noreen, perhaps it's none of our business," Mary Agnes said.

"Of course it is! That heathen should have been strung up long ago. Now he's violated this poor woman and who knows what he did to that poor child in the other room."

Samantha gasped and stood up. "Are you talking about

Patrick? How dare you call him a heathen? He found me half dead in the mountains. He gave both Brian and me food, shelter, and his protection."

Noreen's eyes narrowed. "Just how long have you been living with him?"

"Why?"

Noreen's gaze swept up and down Samantha. "I guess you don't need the help of a good Christian woman." She shook her head. "You really stayed there willingly? Didn't it occur to you how wrong it was? Good women do not stay in the same house as an Indian. You were up there alone with him for God knows how long. You aren't carrying his child are you?"

"Listen lady, I don't know who you think you are. What gives you the right to judge whether I'm a good woman or not? I have done nothing wrong, and neither has Patrick."

"Of course not," Mary Agnes said as she took Samantha's hand. "Sit back down before you fall over. Noreen, perhaps it's best if you leave."

Noreen's eyes narrowed into a bold glare as her lips pressed into a thin line. "This is the very reason I don't like to associate with you, Mary. There are rules to society and you never bother to learn them. Is it any wonder you have never married?"

A rotund man with thinning hair and glasses walked into the room. "Now, ladies, this is not good for either the mother or son."

"Doctor, you may want to know the circumstances before you care for this one or her son. They've been living on the mountain with the half-breed Patrick." Noreen smirked at Mary Agnes.

"Ma'am, I'm Dr. Hanks. Are you well enough to come see your son? He's awake."

She pushed up out of the chair. "Please."

He guided her with his hand at her elbow and they went into his office. Brian's blue eyes were a welcome sight. She took long strides and leaned down, kissing his cheek. "Brian."

He gave her a weary lopsided smile.

"He has a fever and I do believe his hand is the culprit. I don't expect him to stay awake long. I'd like to reopen that hand, though, and see. I think it's best."

"Of course." Relief filled her and tears started pouring down her face. She gently brushed back Brian's hair off his forehead. "Oh, Brian you came back to me."

"Where's Patrick?"

"He sent us ahead on Ahern. I expect he'll be here soon. He'll be so happy you're awake."

"Ahern brought me here?"

"He sure did, and he was proud to do it. I think he remembered how good you are to him."

"I think so too." Brian smiled then his eyes closed.

Doctor Hanks touched her shoulder. "How are you? Any ailments I should know about?"

"Nothing a little warmth can't take care of. I wasn't sure we'd make it."

"You might ask her if she's with child," Noreen said as she put her hand on the door latch. She shook her head and marched out the door.

Her heart plummeted. Patrick hadn't exaggerated how the town's people felt about him. "I, we never…"

"Don't you pay any mind to that biddy," Mary Agnes said. "I'm sure you have a long, interesting tale to tell, but for now I think you should come with me. I have a room you can use."

"That's very kind of you, but I want to stay with Brian."

The door swung open and to her surprise Stinky Sullivan barged right in. "Samantha, so it is you. Where the hell did you get the brat?"

"It's her son," Dr. Hanks said.

"Hell no, she ain't got no brats. She was my intended until she stole everything from the wagon train and took off. I looked for her but I never did find her."

Mary Agnes took a step back. "You were part of the Chigger wagon train? You survived?"

"I was thrown off the train. They left me for dead."

"I'm so glad to see you, sweetheart. Now if you just give back all the money and the land deeds, I'm sure we can figure somethin' out." Stinky threw her a wicked smile.

Mary Agnes put her coat on and left without a word. Dr. Hanks' eyes narrowed on her. "I'm not sure what's going on but we have a young'un that needs medical attention. Is he or isn't he your son?"

"I done told you. She ain't got any children. Where have you been? I thought for sure you was dead." Stinky asked, taking a step forward.

Samantha took a step back until her back was to the wall. "It was you and Chigger who stole the money and led those people—are they all dead? All of them? How did you survive, Stinky?"

"Don't act so surprised. I think you got yourself thrown off the train on purpose. Funny how you found a warm place to hole up while the rest froze. Just tell me where you hid all the money. The land deeds you stole aren't even in your name."

"Don't you come near me. Those deeds were worthless. Chigger sold land that wasn't for sale. As for the money, maybe you can tell me where you hid it? My parents died along the trail, if you remember. Did I make that happen too?"

"Did you?" A booming voice asked and Samantha turned her head. The sheriff stood just inside the door. She hadn't even noticed him come in.

"I hope you're the voice of reason in this town, Sheriff. I don't want this man near me."

The tall, broad shouldered man stared at her, taking her measure. "I'm Sheriff Todd, Ma'am. Those are some big accusations you two are throwing around. We're still trying to figure out what happened to the Chigger party."

"Nice to meet you. I'm Samantha Foley. I was a part of the wagon train but I was put off. My ma died of sickness and my dad fell off his horse and was dragged. My dad and Stinky were going to be partners of some sort. My dad bought land from Mr. Chigger and he had the deed hidden in the wagon along with what money he had. I wasn't allowed to get my stuff from the wagon. They threw me my coat, scarf, a canteen and enough food for one or two days. I tried to follow but they threw rocks at me. One hit me pretty hard in the head and all the blood scared me. I stopped following after that." She took a deep breath. She couldn't gauge if the sheriff believed her or not. "A winter storm hit and I wandered for a bit, sure I was going to die when a trapper named Patrick McCrery found me. He saved my life."

"The boy?"

She swallowed hard. "He was hiding in Patrick's barn. He had run away from a man named Solomon."

The sheriff nodded. "We had a report of a missing boy and a few reports about a man called Solomon. Why is the boy here?"

"He cut his hand and we had to cauterize it. It wouldn't stop bleeding. Soon after he had a fever and didn't wake up."

The sheriff took his tan hat off and slapped it against his thigh. He ran his hand through his thick wavy brown hair. "You came alone?"

"No, Not all the way. Patrick was with us the first day of the trip but we weren't making good enough time so he put me on his horse and told me he'd meet us here." Her heart sank. Why was she being questioned?

"I saw Ahern and figured McCrery was around somewhere. Sullivan, leave the lady alone. She has a sick child."

"It ain't hers."

"She's been taking care of him so I figure she cares enough for him. The child has no one else." The sheriff lifted his right brow. "Go, she's not going anywhere."

Stinky gave her an evil glare. "I'll be watching you." He turned and brushed past the doctor and slammed the door behind him.

"Thank you. I didn't take any money."

He nodded. "I didn't expect so, but that's the story he told when he came riding into town as the only survivor."

"Mr. Chigger died too? I thought he had a place in the mountains," she said.

"That little fact I didn't know about. You watch yourself with Patrick."

She opened her mouth to protest.

"I mean, not yourself but yourself if you're near him. People in this town just don't take to him and some have been downright mean and nasty. Do you have any kin I should notify? Any place you could go come spring?"

"I, I had hoped to find a job here in town." Her voice faded. She could tell by his expression, there probably wouldn't be a job for her.

"You take care of the boy and when you see Patrick tell him he can stay at the old homestead if he wants."

Her eyes widened. "I will thank you."

He gave her a quick smile, placed his hat back on his head, nodded to the doctor and left.

"Looks like you've caused quite a stir."

"I suppose so. Is it alright if I stay by Brian's side tonight?"

Instead of answering, he brought a rocking chair and put

it next to Brian's bed. He grabbed a pillow and blanket for her. "I have food on the stove. I'll be right back."

"Thank you." She sat down, drew the blanket up around her, and drifted off to sleep.

Her hair spilled over her shoulders and he would have thought her an angel except her face pinched around her lips. Patrick glanced at Brian and some of his worry faded. The boy rested peacefully and his breathing was even. He'd run into Sheriff Todd on his way in and knew they'd made it to the doc's place.

Doc Hanks came into the office from his living area and nodded to him. "We'll open that hand up tomorrow. Ya were right to bring him to town."

"Thanks for taking care of them."

Doc nodded toward the other room. "Come, I have food. I knew you weren't far behind."

Patrick smiled. Doc Hanks patched him up plenty over the years. He always had a meal he was willing to share with a scrawny child. "Samantha?" He followed the doctor into the next room.

"She's fine. You wrapped her up well. They both came through the cold unscathed. Sounds like you've had a busy winter up there in those mountains of yours."

"Busiest I've ever known." He sat at the old wooden table and accepted the cup of coffee doc handed him. "Thanks."

Next, the doc handed him a bowl of stew. "What are you planning on doing with those two?"

"Doing?"

"Well, Noreen was already here, as was Mary Agnes. Noreen got her nose bent out of shape when she found out Samantha has been staying with you. Then a fella named Sullivan showed up, claiming the gal as his intended who ran off with the Chigger train's money. Mary left when the sheriff showed up." He poured himself a cup of coffee and sat across from Patrick.

"All this happened already? What's your take on Sullivan? Is Chigger around?"

"No one but Sullivan showed up from the train. He said they all froze to death. Now he claims your gal stole money and land deeds."

His heart squeezed at doc's words. Samantha would never be his gal. "Did he mention Samantha before today?"

"Not that I know of. Never mentioned money or land deeds neither. Now the boy, he was reported missing from an orphanage, I think. The sheriff said something about a Solomon character, but I was busy with the boy."

"It's a complicated story. Solomon grabbed Brian in Denver and practically starved the child. Solomon is dead." He finished the last of his stew. "Ya finally learned to cook."

"You never complained. I have a new widow lady who makes me meals." He smiled.

"Now that wouldn't be Jane Stoop, would it?"

The doctor turned red. "Maybe it is and maybe it isn't."

Patrick laughed deeply, stopping when Samantha stood in the doorway. Their gazes locked and he held his breath, not knowing what to expect. She smiled sweetly at him.

"You made it."

"I did. I see the doc here has taken good care of ya."

"Yes, and Brian is getting better already." Her gaze never left his and he wanted to get lost in her beautiful blue eyes.

"Best news I've heard in awhile. It's late and I need to get out to the homestead."

"You're welcome to bunk here," doc offered.

Finally drawing his gaze away, he glanced at doc. "We've

stirred up enough gossip for one day. I'll be back in the morning."

"Have it your way. I have an extra bedroom, Samantha, if you'd like to lie down."

"The chair is fine."

"Well, I'll leave you two. I need my rest."

"Goodnight," Samantha said as the doc climbed the stairs. "How far away is the homestead?"

"Not far. I'll be fine."

She nodded, shifting her weight from one foot to the other.

He stood and walked to her, embracing her tight. "I was worried about ya," he murmured.

"I was worried about you too. I'm glad you're here. There are things going on."

"I heard about Sullivan. Don't worry about it. Ya get some sleep. I have a feeling tomorrow will be a trying day. Are ya warm enough here?"

She pulled out of his arms just enough to look up at him. "I've never had anyone worry about me the way you do, except for my parents. You won't leave town without me?"

"I won't leave ya in a lurch." It was as evasive as he could get. He kissed her on the forehead and grabbed his coat hat and rifle. "I'll see ya in the morning."

The homestead wasn't far and Ahern had done enough for one day. Patrick started his trek out of town. Sheriff Todd said he'd light a fire in the place so at least it would be warm. He didn't know why he hung on to the property. Perhaps it was the only thing he'd gotten from his father. Shrugging, he sighed. At least he had a place to sleep for the night. Tomorrow would bring new troubles; he had no doubt about it.

The place was solid but in general disrepair. The log cabin stood strong but the porch sagged and the steps looked none too safe. He opened the door and the fire pulled at him. It'd be good to be warm for a change. Looking around he shook his head. There were many bad times in this cabin but there were some nice times, while his mother was alive. He pulled the sheets off the fine furniture. His father was always trying to impress others, but no one cared.

He made his way into the bedroom and practically fell into bed he was so tired.

CHAPTER EIGHT

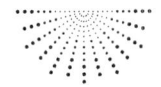

*S*amantha woke with a start and for a second she didn't know where she was but as soon as she saw Brian's eyes open, she smiled. "Good morning."

"Good morning. How'd I get here? I thought town was a long way off." His brow furrowed as he stared at her.

"It took a few days to get you here. Your hand is infected. The doctor wants to operate on it today—"

Brian quickly sat up and swung his legs over the side of the bed. "No way is any saw bones gonna take my hand off. I'll die like a man with both hands attached."

Standing she put her hands on his shoulders. "Stay in bed. No one is cutting your hand off."

"At least not today. You must be Brian." Dr. Hanks smiled as he shook Brian's hand. "There's a bucket behind the screen there you can use."

"No outhouse?"

"Sure it's right out back but it's cold out there."

"I ain't no baby who needs a bucket." He jutted his chin out.

Samantha and Dr. Hanks exchanged glances. "Fine, but I'm walking you out there. I can't have you fainting on me."

Brian nodded, jumped out of bed, grabbed his shoes and ran out the back door.

"He seems to be doing better today," the doctor said with a smile. "Be right back."

The weight crushing her chest lifted and she could breathe for the first time in days. She had faith Brian would be fine. She walked into the kitchen and began to make breakfast. She scrambled the eggs and got biscuits ready to go.

The door opened and she turned to smile at Brian and the doctor but a lovely blonde haired blue-eyed woman stood right inside the door. Her hair was up with wispy tendrils framing her heart shaped face. She held a big basket in her hands.

"Hello," Samantha said.

"Yes, hello indeed. And you are?" She wasn't smiling.

"I'm Samantha. I brought a young boy here last night. Looks like surgery is planned for today."

"I'm Jane Stoop. I fix the meals for the doctor. All of his meals." Her voice was a complete contrast to her sweet appearance.

"Sorry, I didn't know. He's been so kind, I thought I'd make him breakfast." She touched the back of her head and realized most of her hair had escaped her bun.

"Where did you sleep last night?" Jane's eyes narrowed.

"In a rocking chair next to Brian." She didn't like the way Jane stared at her as if she'd done something wrong.

"Is that a fact?"

"Yes it is. Hello, Jane." Dr. Hanks followed Brian into the house, walked across the room and gave Jane a kiss on the cheek. He glanced at each woman and frowned. "Is something amiss?"

"I thought I'd make breakfast to thank you."

"Jane's not used to anyone else in my kitchen, but I do thank you. I need to explain the procedure to Brian. I'm sure you can work it out." His lips twitched as he gestured for Brian to follow him to his office.

"Why, he hardly looked at you. I mean, I thought, well you're very pretty."

Samantha shook her head. "I'm just plain me. I'm not looking for a husband. I have all I can handle right now."

"Tell you what, we can work together and you can tell me how you came to be here."

Smiling, Samantha placed the biscuits in the oven. "It's so nice not having to cook over a fire for a change."

"How'd you end up here?"

"Brian cut his hand. Patrick and I tried to seal the wound but it got infected anyway. We came down the mountain." She put the cast-iron pan on the burner.

"Patrick? Mountain Man Patrick? Oh my, you poor dear. You're safe now and I think talking to another woman about your trials will help." Jane sat down and waited.

"There were no trials. Patrick rescued me from the cold mountains and did the same for Brian."

"But something must have happened. How long have you been with him?"

Samantha turned her back to Jane. Just another busybody hoping for a vivacious story. Why couldn't people believe in the good of people instead of instantly jumping to conclusions and judgement? She cooked the bacon and was silent for a while. "A few months I suppose."

"Months? You do know he's an Indian, don't you?"

"Why does that matter?" Her spine stiffened.

"Oh you poor lamb. You're soiled goods now."

She turned and glared at Jane. "What does that mean?"

"Oh, you know, a white man would never take you for his

wife. No one will hire you. Maybe Braney down at the saloon would make you one of his girls. You are pretty enough."

Gasping, she brought her hand to her throat. She felt a cold breeze and there stood Patrick looking thunderous. He pointedly ignored Jane. "How's Brian?"

"Well enough to refuse to use a bucket and went out to the necessary instead."

Laughing, he locked gazes with her. "Good. It should help with the surgery. How did ya sleep?"

"I slept in the chair."

"I know that. I asked how not where."

Her face heated. "Sorry. I slept fairly well and was overjoyed when I woke up to Brian staring at me."

His face softened. "Ya keep that joy inside ya and don't let anyone take it from ya."

"Thank you. I will. Breakfast is about ready. Would you join us?"

Jane's jaw dropped open.

"Thank ya. I'm hungry."

She smiled. "Good. Go tell Dr. Hanks and Brian to wash up."

As soon as Patrick left the room, Jane crossed to stand toe to toe with Samantha. "I refuse to eat with him. A proper lady would not share a meal with an Indian."

"Well I guess you can take your basket and don't let the door hit your backside as you leave."

Jane's eyes widened. She put her hands on her hips and her lips thinned into a grim line. "You're digging your own hole. I don't know who you are or where you're from but I'll find out. You better hope that man takes you back up the mountain with him." She turned on her booted heel, grabbed her coat and basket and slammed the door shut behind her.

Dr. Hanks peered around the corner. "I was afraid she'd act that way. Sorry."

"It's not your fault. Come, let's eat while the food is hot. What about Brian? Should he eat?"

"I have him lying down. Ether tends to make a person sick to their stomach so I think we'll hold off. Don't worry, he'll be fine. The fever is down and that was my main concern when you brought him here."

Nodding, she placed platters of eggs, bacon, and biscuits on the table. Patrick joined them and they all ate. She was too lost in thought to notice the silence at first, but both men seemed to have things on their minds too. Brian was going to be just fine. She didn't care what the other people in the town said. It didn't matter. She just needed Brian healthy.

"I'm going to need your help, Samantha. Since Jane left, I'll need an assistant."

Perspiration formed on her brow but she nodded.

"You too, Patrick. He should hold still but just in case."

"I'd be glad to."

The doctor nodded. "Okay, we might as well get started."

THE FEAR in Brian's eyes made his gut clench. If he could, he'd take all the pain for Brian, but all he could do was help. "You'll be just fine."

Brian stared at him with trust in his eyes. "I know. You won't leave, will you?"

"I'll be here when you wake up."

Satisfied, Brian nodded. "Ready."

Samantha smiled down on him, brushed a lock of hair from his forehead and gave him a quick kiss. "See you when you wake up."

The doctor started the ether until Brian fell under and handed it over to Samantha. "I've done this before," she assured them.

"Patrick, just hold his arm still. I'm going to cut now."

The smell of blood filled the air and Samantha swayed slightly before she righted herself and took a deep breath.

"It's puss filled. I'll just clean it all out."

Patrick stared at her until she looked up at him. She gave him a slight smile. They stared at each other until the last stitch was finished.

"That should do it."

Patrick finally took a deep breath. "Thanks, doc." He watched as the doctor wrapped Brian's hand.

"Why don't you two go sit in my parlor. I have some cleaning to do in here."

"I'll help," Samantha offered.

Dr. Hanks shook his head. "I have certain procedures, go, sit."

"If you're sure?"

"Patrick, take your woman and go sit by the fire."

He held out his hand and was rewarded with a smile as she took it. *His woman,* if only it could be true. Her small hand felt cold in his and he pulled her along into the other room. "Sit down, and I'll get the coffee."

"Sounds good." She gave him a long, lingering look and it caused his heart to speed up. She affected him just by being near him. Being back in town reinforced his decision to leave her here.

"I'm glad it went okay. Someone must be looking out for him. He's certainly been through a lot." He poured the coffee and handed one of the filled cups to her. He sat in a chair next to her and took a swig of the coffee. "If it wasn't for that shrew, Jenny, I'd say ya and the doc would make a great pair. The sheriff is a great guy."

She put her coffee on the table, stood, and with rigid posture, she walked to the window. She crossed her arms in front of her and stared out at the cold day. He knew her by now, she was mad. The tapping of her foot was the only sound. She was more than mad.

"Not talking to me?" A long pause followed.

"No, I mean yes. You're not taking us back with ya." It was a statement rather than a question and he winced.

"It's for the best."

She whirled around and stared at him. "Best for who? I don't think anyone in this town will give me a job. Where will I live?" Her eyes flashed at him, then she shrugged. "I'm sorry, it's not your problem. I'm not your problem. You've been more than generous to Brian and me. I understand your concerns, but I don't agree with them." She gave him a wobbly smile before she turned back to the window.

Running his hand through his hair, he tried to think of an answer. There had to be something he could say to make the situation better, but no matter how hard he tried, he couldn't come up with anything. "I'm sorry."

She nodded and her posture stiffened once again. "I'll figure something out. After I got kicked off the wagon train, I swore all people to be evil, except my parents of course. You proved to me that there is still goodness in the world. I'll look for the goodness and I'm sure I'll be fine."

"I'll bring ya out to the homestead tomorrow. Ya can live there and I'll make sure it's fully stocked. Both ya and Brian will be comfortable there." He tried to sound positive but he wasn't sure if his words were true. They'd have a roof over their heads and food to eat. Come spring they could move to another town.

"Th-thank you." Her voice shook.

"Brian is waking."

Samantha left him behind as she hurried into the other room. She was upset now but eventually she'd realize it was all for the best. She may think she wanted to be with him, but eventually she'd find life was not all roses being tied to him. He wanted more for her and Brian. They deserved happiness and he was sure to bring them nothing but heartache.

"Thanks, doc. I appreciate it."

"I heard part of your conversation. Are you really planning to leave her? You'd be a jackass if you did. She loves you. I see it every time she looks at you. You love her back."

"That may be true, but being married to me would end in disaster. No one would accept her and what about the boy? I know what it feels like to be shunned by this community. I won't put them through it." He stiffened as he felt the usual loneliness run through him. It was a feeling he'd have for the rest of his life. "Tell Samantha I'll be back tomorrow to take her to the homestead." He grabbed his coat and hat and was out the door before he put them on.

Life was all about making sacrifices. Sometimes they were your choice but other times it was what had to be. Brian would be fine and Samantha was strong. In a few years, they'd forget about him, but he knew he'd never forget. He'd never forget the feel of her in his arms or the taste of her sweet lips. It was just as well, he never intended to bring a child of his into an unforgiving world. His body was scarred enough and he'd not allow the same thing to happen to his children.

He shrugged into his coat, donned his hat and began his trudge through the snow. He didn't get far before his way was blocked by three unsavory looking men. "Whatever it is ya think ya want, ya don't. Just let me by."

"You the Injun Sammy's been shacking up with?" The man was tall and he had the look of the devil in his eye. He sneered. "I bet you know where the money is. In fact I bet you know a whole lot about Sammy."

Patrick widened his stance ready for anything. "Stinky Sullivan? You're exactly as she described. A piece of filth."

"Why you…" Stinky pulled out a knife.

"Put it down!" A voice behind Patrick demanded. "You have been nothing but trouble since you came to town." The Sheriff stepped between the two men. "Patrick is a friend of mine and I'd take it more than personally if anything happened to him." He pointed his finger at Sullivan. "Do you understand?"

"He's just an Injun," Stinky grumbled.

"I want all harassment of Patrick and Miss Foley to stop. There is no evidence she stole the money from the wagon train."

"Was Chigger ever found?" Patrick asked, eyeing Sullivan.

"Not hide nor hair."

"I have a suspicion as to where he's holed up," Patrick said.

Stinky Sullivan's eyes widened in fear. "He ain't dead?"

"Guess he didn't let you in on his scheme."

"We were partners! I thought they were all dead."

Patrick narrowed his eyes. "Just how exactly did ya survive? There's a lot of territory between this town and where the wagons probably got stuck."

"I was sent to find help."

The sheriff crossed his arms in front of him and cocked his eyebrow. "And?"

"And what?"

"And did you find help? I can't say anyone asked me for any. It wasn't until I got a telegram saying the train never arrived that I began to ask around. You said you were the lone survivor."

Sullivan's weight shifted from one leg to the other. The other two men gradually took steps back until they turned and walked away. "I thought I was until Sammy showed up."

"It'll be a few months before we can venture out that way. I doubt there will be much of anything left when we do find it." The sheriff glanced at Patrick. "Don't you think?"

"I know that little gal didn't have any money on her—I picked her up in my arms and I would have noticed any extra weight. I believe her story. Chigger might have left the poor folks to their death and taken the money or maybe ya have the money, Sullivan." Patrick took a step toward the other man.

"You have no proof of nothin'." He turned on his heel and stomped away.

"A lot going on up on that mountain of yours."

"Too much."

"You still planning to leave soon?"

"Maybe tomorrow. It's my decision."

"I know it is. See ya around and watch your back. I don't trust Sullivan."

Patrick nodded. "Me neither."

IT'D BEEN another sleepless night. The doc offered her a bed but she wanted to sit by Brian. His color was good and there was no sign of a fever. Part of her burdened heart was lightened. The other part would be forever buried she was afraid. It was shocking to have the townspeople treat her so badly. She'd been raised in a nice community with people who had good manners. Patrick had warned her, but she never fathomed such hatefulness.

Then there was the biggest burden, Patrick. He didn't want her. He didn't need her and if she was being truthful, he was trying to get away from her. Sure, he cared for her but not enough to ask her to be his wife. She remembered asking her mother how you knew when you found love. Her mother told her she'd feel it. She felt it till it hurt so deeply she wasn't sure she could bear it.

Patrick was a hero and people treated him like dirt. He saved both her and Brian but they didn't care. She longed to run off into the mountains with him, but now she had Brian to consider. It would affect how people viewed him and it could damage any future he hoped to have. She sighed. It wasn't her choice. Patrick didn't want her with him.

Brian stirred and opened his eyes. He smiled. "My hand is still there. I thought for sure that sawbones would cut it off."

"You're going to be just fine. Patrick will be here soon to take us to his homestead."

"Really? We're going to live near town? Maybe I can make some friends and have my own horse!"

"He plans to leave Ahern with us so the horse part is already taken care of."

His smile faded. "He's going back to his cabin? Alone?"

Blinking back a few tears, she tried to smile. "Yes, he is, and he offered us a place to live. I'm so very grateful for his kindness."

Brian stared at her until she finally glanced away. Somehow, she needed to make it seem like a good thing. "I bet there are a lot of boys your age around."

"Did he already leave? Will I get a chance to say goodbye?" The anxiousness in his voice tore at her.

"He said he'd take us to the homestead."

"And I will," Patrick said. He leaned against the doorway into the living quarters with a cup of coffee in his hands. "I came in the back door in case ya were sleeping."

"You're here!" Brian tried to sit up, then groaned as he put his head back down.

"Take it easy. Of course, I'm here. I'm going to take ya to a place I own."

"Why don't you live there?" Brian asked.

"Didn't suit me." He sipped his coffee.

She drank in the sight of him. Time was getting short and she may never see him again. His brawny shoulders filled the doorway. His legs were long and strong and his hands so capable. He was strong and hard when needed and he was a gentle man. She longed to stroke his neatly trimmed beard, and the memory of how his mustache tickled when they kissed caused her to blush. By the time she got to his slate blue eyes she could tell by the twinkle in them, he was well aware of her perusal. She couldn't tear her gaze away for this was a memory she needed to carry in her heart. He was the one, just as her mother told her, she just knew it. Her hopes for her future dashed. They'd be saying goodbye soon.

"I'll just freshen up and we can be on our way." She stood and as she walked by him, he touched her hand. She kept walking, not knowing what to do or say. Her instinct had been to grab it and ask him to take them back with him, but she had her pride. She went upstairs to the spare room and got her things ready. Looking in the mirror, she cringed. She looked beyond tired but there was no help for it. She brushed her hair, took a deep breath and walked back down the stairs.

He stood at the bottom of the staircase, his gaze drinking her in as she had just done to him. He knew what he was walking away from. Her heart ached. He knew and was going to do it anyway.

They bundled themselves and Brian up and went outside. The wind had stopped and for a moment. The sun on the snow shimmered beautifully. It reminded her of fool's gold, maybe because she felt like a fool. She wasn't sure. It wasn't a long walk at all and the house was surprisingly nice. She'd pictured a rundown structure but it appeared sturdy. "It looks nice."

"Thanks. I've had it a long while. I just never got around

to selling it. I've rented it out on occasion." He carried Brian up the front steps, opened the door and gestured for her to precede him.

"It's homey." She glanced around and all the nice touches surprised her. There were red and white checked curtains with a matching tablecloth. There were even enough chairs around the table. "A wood stove? I can cook anything on a stove." She smiled and then as she remembered he'd be leaving her smile faded.

"I like it." Brian announced from the spot on the couch where Patrick laid him.

"It'll be warm and you'll be safe. There's enough supplies to last five months or so."

"Surely, winter won't last that long." Every muscle in her body tensed.

"I wasn't sure how long ya intended to stay." He took his hat off and ran his fingers through his hair. "The people might warm up to ya or ya might want to continue on West. I told Mrs. Andrews over at the general store to put anything ya might need on my bill. Of course, I'll leave Ahern with ya. He's out back in the barn. Brian you'll take good care of him, won't ya?"

"You bet! Wish you were staying though."

"Me too, buddy, me too." He pulled Brian to his side and gave Brian a quick hug. The sad expressions on both of their faces tugged at her heart.

"Well…" She didn't know what to say. Asking him to stay would do no good, and he didn't want them on the mountain with him. It was as though a part of her was being ripped away.

"I'm not good at goodbyes. Ya take care of yourself and I hope everything works out the way ya want it. Ya deserve to be happy. If you're still here next time I come to town, I'll stop in and check on ya." His gaze held hers and for a split second, she thought she saw regret.

"Thank you for everything. You should probably go. I'm not good at goodbyes either." Her smile quivered.

"Take care." He gave her one last glance, waved at Brian and walked out the door, taking her heart with him.

"I wish we could go with him."

"Me too, Brian, me too."

CHAPTER NINE

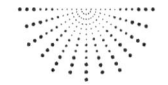

Three months later

Samantha sat on the front porch sewing clothes and watching Brian kick an empty can around the yard. He'd grown sadder by the day and she wasn't sure what to do. The rest of the children in town wouldn't play with him. It wasn't any better for her. She tried everything to get the people to accept her. She and Brian went to church each Sunday, only to be ignored. She'd hoped the preacher would intervene but he pretended not to notice. She tried to start up conversations with people while she was at the store, but people turned and walked away. She even tried to make money by doing laundry, but she had no customers.

The only people who were kind to her were the sheriff and the doctor. They were busy men and not ones to talk a lot. Each rebuff hurt, but she kept trying for Brian's sake. School would be starting and she wanted him to attend, but she was afraid of how he'd be treated.

Stinky Sullivan was still in town but for some reason he hadn't continued to accuse her of theft. From what she'd seen, he spent his waking moments at the saloon gambling.

She made sure their paths never crossed. A time or two he came barreling toward her and she hurried to the other side of the street, escaping him. The thunderous looks he gave her scared her. Maybe she needed to carry a gun.

"Sam, do I have ta go to school? You already taughted me a lot," Brian pleaded. He was nervous and afraid but it was in his best interest.

"It's taught, not taughted and yes you have to go. All children go to school. You like to read and you're quick at math. Just think of all the things you'll learn."

"No, I just need you. You'll be here when I get out of school, won't you?"

Her heart melted. "Of course I'll be here, Brian. I wouldn't dream of leaving you."

"I think I've been with you the longest, well, except for the orphanage, but I don't remember it much. I was too little. I do remember I hated it."

"Well, we have each other and that's all that matters."

"Do you think Patrick will come down the mountain?" His eyes widened with hope.

She shook her head. "I don't know, Brian." He nodded and went back to kicking the can. She wished she could tell him Patrick would come to see them but in truth, he'd been to town once already and never contacted her. A more intense hurt she'd never known. In a superficial way, she understood his leaving them in town but deep down she held on to the hope of their love. But what did she know? She'd never known love for a man before. Perhaps it was easier for a man to turn away from his feelings.

She stood up, went back into the house, and poured herself a glass of water. Her father grieved deeply for her mother. The same doubts ran through her daily, but she had easily shrugged them off until the woman at the mercantile told her Patrick had been in. It'd been as though someone had pushed all the air out of her and it left her gasping while Noreen Black and Mrs. Andrews gaped at her.

Patrick hadn't reordered supplies for them, not that they were his responsibility but panic had begun to set in. She needed a job. The saloon was her only option. Maybe it was time to leave town. Time for a new beginning. Hearing Brian talking to someone, she hurried outside.

Her hand went to her neck and her jaw dropped. "Mr. Chigger? Where are the rest of the people?"

The older, unkempt man laughed, showing his brown teeth. "I don't think there are any other people who survived. I figured you for dead and that Sullivan fella never came back. He probably froze to death."

"You'll find Stinky in the saloon. He's there every day gambling."

"Gambling?" He stroked his long white beard. "Now I know what happened to all the money from those poor souls who perished in the snow."

Her eyes narrowed. "Where exactly have you been?"

"There's a bunch of trappers up there in them mountains. A couple of them found me and I laid up with them."

"Well if you survived, surely there must be others?"

"No, Ma'am. I went to find help, and when I returned they were all dead and half eaten by wolves."

She cringed. "I see. Come on, Brian, we need to get inside."

"I don't rightly remember you having a child."

"I didn't. Good day."

She put her arm around Brian's shoulder and hurried inside. Chigger was lying and she hadn't liked the way he looked at her as if she was a problem he needed to get rid of. Hopefully he'll concentrate on Sullivan and the money. Maybe he'd leave her alone. She needed to be sure all the guns were loaded. Something bad was about to happen, she could feel it. The saloon it would be.

After Brian went to bed that evening, she took a long bath. Too bad it wasn't a soothing one. Tense muscles and nerve racking thoughts of Braney, the saloon owner, kept her from enjoying anything. Finally, she got out of the bath, dried herself off and put her nightgown on. It took her a while to empty all the water out and by the time she finished she was exhausted.

The next day the sun rose in glorious colors of pink and blue, combining in places to make purple until it finally changed to its fiery yellow splendor. The birds all sang and she wished she too had a song in her heart. She had just finished making a stack of pancakes when Brian sat down at the table.

"I don't like that man." he said the edges of his mouth turned downward.

"What man?"

"That Chigger fella. He's sitting outside on the front porch as if he owns the place. I found him there after I fed Ahern. I told him to leave and he said I have bad manners." His frown turned deeper.

The chair scraped across the floor when she stood. "You stay here. I need to have a talk with Mr. Chigger."

"Sam, I don't think you should go out there. He's a mean one."

"It'll be fine, you'll see." Grabbing her shawl, she wrapped it around her as she walked out the door. Brian was right, Chigger sat in one of the handmade chairs on the porch. From the smell of him, she guessed he spent his night in the saloon.

"I was wonderin' how long it'd take you to come out." His deep voice sent a shiver down her spine.

"What is it you want?" She bit the inside of her cheek,

trying to keep her face expressionless. It wouldn't do to have him know she was frightened.

"I want my money, for starters. Stinky says you had it on you when we left you for dead."

"So you admit you didn't plan on me surviving."

"I admit nothing. Just give me the money and I'll go away."

She itched to slap the smirk off his face. "I don't have any money. Did you ask Stinky how he could afford to gamble every night?"

Chigger slowly shook his head. "He said you'd say that. Fact is, Ol' Stinky has been on a winning streak unlike anything I've ever seen. He's one lucky son of a bitch."

Crossing her arms in front of her, she stared at him. "You really believe that? I thought you were smarter than that. I think you know I'm telling you the truth. It wasn't my idea to leave the train. But if I remember right, it was both you and Stinky's idea I marry Tom. I always thought it a bit strange. I think the money was in my wagon. I think Stinky put it in there for when it all came up missing—no one would have suspected my father of stealing. I know I can't blame my mother's death on you, but you were out hunting with my father when he was killed." She walked down the porch steps, anxious to put space between them. "You left me for dead afterward. I don't know why I didn't put it all together until now."

"You little fool. You don't know what you're talking about," Chigger growled. "I made a few inquiries about the boy. The orphanage doesn't like having runaways on their record. Seems they'd be glad to have him back."

She gasped. "I told you I don't have your money!"

Chigger stood and walked down the steps. "I know you don't. I knew it all along. I just wanted to see what you knew. You see, it ain't healthy for me to have you around." He tipped his hat, mounted his horse and rode away without looking back.

The shock of his words paralyzed her. What was she going to do? Staying was no longer an option and she was out of choices. They'd have to pack lightly and make it to the next town. Her heart squeezed painfully. The only way to do it was to take Ahern with them. Hopefully Patrick would understand.

Still sick to her stomach, she turned and strode to the house. The quicker they left the better.

"What do you mean she's gone?" Patrick roared as he stared at Sheriff Todd. He'd come to town to restock Samantha and Brian's supplies and found a note on the old kitchen table.

"A couple days ago. She packed up and off they went." The sheriff leaned his chair back on two legs until he hit the wall behind him. "I told her it was a mistake but she told me she needed to keep Brian safe. I asked what the problem was but she refused to talk. I couldn't keep her here."

Exasperated, Patrick loudly sighed. "Her note didn't say why, just she was sorry she had to take Ahern. Hell, the horse is the least of my problems. Someone threatened her."

"My thoughts exactly. I think it was Chigger, but she wouldn't say. How can you protect a person when they won't say?" He righted his chair with a thud.

"Chigger is here? Oh hell!" His eyebrows shot up and his gut clenched. It wasn't any wonder she took off. "Got a horse I can borrow?"

"Take Snowstorm. Tell Jonnie at the livery I said it was a good thing."

"A good thing?"

The sheriff smiled. "Code words. Means it's official business and to let you have the horse. People think my job can be easy but if you need a posse fast, you need horses fast too. The code words were my idea."

Patrick barely heard the last words. He was out the door and at the livery in no time. He got Snowstorm, a tall white gelding and stopped at the mercantile. His jaw hurt from gritting his teeth the whole time he gathered supplies. Widow Andrews watched his every move just as she did when he was a child.

"Will this be all?" She asked in a haughty manner.

"Yes."

"Where you going? I see you have that devil of a horse with you." Her eyes narrowed. "Does the sheriff know you have it?"

"How much do I owe ya?" He tried to keep his voice light and even.

"I'll subtract it from the credit you have."

Usually he waited for a total and a bill of sale. He didn't trust the old biddy and he liked to know exactly how much he had in credit. The first time he came down the mountain she tried to cheat him, thinking he couldn't add. "Fine. I'm in a hurry. I'll check with ya when I come back into town for the bill."

Frowning, she gave him a curt nod. She grabbed her feather duster and started dusting some cans, keeping her gaze on him the whole time.

He quickly gathered his things and left. *Damn woman.* There had been so many bad moments of loneliness the past few months and he'd somehow talked himself into asking Samantha to be his wife, but now his thinking was right again. He'd condemn her to a life of nasty injustices and he wasn't going to do it.

He packed his saddlebags and loaded up Snowstorm. Walking back to the rail where the horse was tied, he took a moment to look into the horse's eyes. He stroked his nose and leaned in until their faces touched. Taking a step back, he nodded. Snowstorm would do well.

Mounting, he was soon on his way out of town. He figured she decided to travel to the nearest town. He hoped he was right. She was a capable woman, but there was still danger along the way. They'd already spent two nights away from the homestead. Depending on how far they traveled each day, they could make it by morning. He had a lot of distance to travel.

Thankfully, it wasn't cold during the day. The nights would be fine if they were able to start a fire. What the heck had Chigger done to make her run? He was a mean one and most probably a murderer. The more he thought about it the angrier he got. He should have protected her better. He should have made sure she and Brian were safe. He might not be able to have them for a family, but they were his responsibility.

Leaving them at the homestead seemed to be the right choice, the only choice. Thoughts of her spun him in circles until he didn't know which way was up anymore. He needed to find them and make sure they were safe and had a place to live before going back up his mountain.

Snowstorm's endurance amazed him and they covered a lot of ground. The sun was quickly setting and he planned to keep going as long as he could. He jumped down and took the reins, leading the horse through the trail. He couldn't take a chance of Snowstorm stepping into an unseen hole and getting hurt. They stopped many times and rested. Finally, he stopped and leaning against a tree, he slept.

Up before the sun, he quickly ate and was off again. He traveled through a heavily treed area and he felt the change in the air. He could smell a storm coming. As he rode into a clearing, he gazed up at the sky and swore. The clouds were black, blue, and filled with rain. The wind began to pick up and he urged Snowstorm to go a bit faster. Again, he was grateful for the powerful horse.

Large drops began to fall. Patrick pulled out a blanket to drape over his head and back. The pelts he wore kept a lot of the rain off his skin. It was time to stop and rest. The scream of a mountain lion raised the hair on the back of his neck. He grabbed his rifle and got off the horse. Ahern started to race by him but he slowed when he spotted Patrick. *Damn, where were Samantha and Brian?*

The cry of the lion echoed through the air and he began to run toward it. He was almost out of breath when he finally spotted them. They were in a good position in a cave above the ground. Samantha stood at the entrance with her rifle aimed at the mangy cat. He didn't hesitate; he aimed and shot. The mountain lion dropped and lay still.

Samantha's eyes grew wide as she frantically looked around for him. He walked into the clearing as she sagged against the cave wall, tears in her eyes. Quickly he ran to the cave, intent on taking Samantha into his arms but he was tackled by Brian instead. Luckily, he kept his balance as the boy jumped into his arms.

"Damn, it's good to see ya safe."

"Patrick, we missed you. Where have you been? We were almost mountain lion food. Ahern! Did he eat Ahern?"

He patted Brian's back and set him down. A lump formed in his throat as he gazed from one frightened face to the other. "Ahern is just fine. I met him on the trail coming here." He couldn't get enough of staring at Samantha. He looked at her from head to toe, reassuring himself she was fine. Finally, his gaze rested on her lovely face.

Tears rolled down her face as she sagged to the ground, shaking. She appeared so lost and he couldn't stand it. The next thing he knew he was sitting next to her. He drew her into his arms and onto his lap. Immediately she wrapped her arms around his neck and pressed her sweet body against his.

"I'm so glad to see you," she whispered against his neck. "I was ready to shoot but it kept moving. I would have shot it, you know."

"I know." He rocked her as his cheek lay next to hers. The softness of her hair and smoothness of her skin stirred him.

"She would have. Sam is the bravest!" Brian all smiles plopped down next to them. "But I'm glad to see you too. You're like a good luck charm, Patrick. You always save us."

He couldn't help the smile that spread widely across his face. It was a good feeling to be needed. A very good feeling, one he'd wish would never go away. His smile faded. He knew the score.

"How did you know where to find us? We just left town a few days ago," Samantha asked as she pulled out of his arms. She smiled at him and then slid off his lap. She sat in line with them, her back against the wall. Her body still shook.

"Let me get the horses. Brian, can ya come with me and help gather wood for a fire?" He took off his coat, laid it over her and gave her shoulder a soft squeeze. "You'll be okay here?"

She nodded. "Yes. Go, get Ahern. I hate to think of him out there alone."

"We'll be right back." He motioned for Brian to follow him and out into the pouring rain they went.

"The wood will be wet!" Brian yelled above the wind.

"It's dryer in the woods and I have some wrapped in canvas on Snowstorm."

"What? It's going to snow again?" Brian had to run to keep up with him.

Stopping he turned toward Brian. "Snowstorm is a horse, and we'll find dryer wood under the trees."

"Okay!" He ran down the trail.

Patrick shook his head and laughed. It sounded strange to him. He hadn't had much reason to laugh in the last few months. Up ahead he spotted Brian talking to both horses and it looked to be quite the conversation.

"This is the sheriff's horse. If he finds you you'll go to jail and jail ain't no joke."

"That's right it ain't no joke. The sheriff lent the horse to me. This is Snowstorm."

"Okay, I'll get some wood. Sam looks very, very cold. It's been hard on her. She cries at night sometimes. Not just here but back at the house too. I think she misses you and the ladies are mean there. No one likes us." He stared at Patrick, his eyes intense.

"Well, let's get the wood and get back." What was he supposed to say? Brian probably figured he could solve all their problems. He sighed. He'd let the child down again when he left. They collected a bit of wood and headed back to the cave. It wouldn't be enough for the night but it wasn't easy juggling the wood, the horses and Brian all at once. A trip for more wood was in his future.

The mud began to suck his feet down into the earth and walking became difficult. "Almost there," he said to Brian and the horses.

"Sam was real good at making fires for us. She kept us real safe too. Do you think she's pretty? I do. I bet she'd make a great wife." Brian gave him a sidelong glance.

His lips twitched and he wanted to laugh. "She's pretty." He continued walking.

"And she knows how to cook," Brian added, practically running to keep up with Patrick.

The cave came into site and Snowstorm began to pull back on the reins. "It's okay boy, you're fine." He soothed the horse until he was ready to go on.

"What's wrong with him?"

"The smell of blood from the dead mountain lion makes him want to run."

"In the other direction."

"Yes, Brian, in the other direction. Look, there's Samantha waiting for the wood."

"I bet she's real cold."

"I bet she is too, let's go." They walked straight to the cave and dropped off the wood. The appreciation in her eyes warmed him. A man could get used to such things. "I'll go tie up the horses." He escaped into the wet weather. He'd known seeing her again would make his heart hurt even more.

With a lump in his throat, he returned to the cave and squatted down. He placed the smaller canvas covered wood into a circle near the front of the cave. The heat of her gaze warmed him. He smiled as Brian sat next to him, clearly confident a fire would get going any second. He pulled out his flint and lit the dry wood. Before long, a warm blaze lit the inside of the cave. "Ya were lucky to find this place."

"Indeed we were, and just in time for this nasty weather." Her voice washed over him and he wanted to have her in his arms again.

"I'm hungry. We've had a lot of beans, Patrick. Do you have something good in one of your packs?"

Patrick laughed. "I have beans too, Brian. Look in that other bag against the wall. I have dried beef in it."

"I'm not going to be a trapper if I have to eat beans all the time. Sam said cowboys eat lots of beans too."

"Ya take with ya what travels best. Beans ya can eat right out of the can and they're filling. Dried beef takes up almost no room. It just makes sense to me. Now, for instance I could carry canned peaches but they are a bit heavy and don't fill the belly as much."

"Oh, I don't suppose you have any heavy peaches, do ya?"

Samantha smiled. "Brian, we'll be in town in a few days. Maybe I can find you something different to eat." Her smiled faded.

His brow furrowed. "What happened to your smile?" Patrick asked.

"I shouldn't make promises I might not be able to keep. I could try to trade the beans for something else but I'm not sure." She stared at the fire, clasping and unclasping her hands. "We might as well get out of these wet clothes." She stood and began to rummage through her bags. "Here, Brian, put these on." She handed him a set of clothes and grabbed a set for herself.

Standing up straight, she nodded at him. "Thanks to you we have another set of clothes. I don't know how I'll ever be able to thank you."

His throat closed for a second. "Knowing you're safe is thanks enough. Come on Brian, let's turn our backs so Samantha can get dressed."

Her memory didn't do Patrick justice. His shoulders were broader, his hair longer and his eyes kinder than she remembered. He smiled and laughed easier than before. He still had the ability to make her heart race. He was the one person who actually liked her and Brian. Such a stark contrast to the people of the town.

"You look good. How was the rest of the winter in the mountains?"

"Fine, everything was fine. A bit quiet."

"We missed you!" Brian added. "The people in town are mean and one man named Trigger made Sam cry."

"He means Chigger."

"I heard from the sheriff he was back. Just found out." He

gave her a long probing look. "Did he hurt ya?"

"No, nothing like that. He threatened me. First, he played a little game of where is the money. He knew all along Stinky took it. I did accuse him of leading those poor people to their deaths. I'm a witness who knows too much. He said he'd have Brian sent back to the orphanage if I told anyone, but I don't think he intends for me to live." She shivered.

"I asked around and no one knew where he'd holed up all winter. I thought maybe he was dead."

"Unfortunately he's very much alive. I'm not sure moving to the next town will change anything. He can still find me, but maybe people would help me. I just don't know."

"Patrick, people have been mean to Sam and me. They cross the street if they see us coming. The lady at the mercantile sniffs the air when we walk in as if we smell or something. She said you came to town, settled our account and left. How come you came to town and didn't come to see me?"

There was no disguising the pain in his eyes. "The account wasn't settled. I brought more furs down to make sure there was enough money to last ya into next summer."

"And?"

"And what?"

"And why didn't you come to visit me? I thought we were friends." Tears filled Brian's eyes.

Patrick hesitated so long, she wasn't sure he was going to answer Brian's questions.

"Ya know how Mrs. Andrews from the store treats ya? If I had been with ya, she would have treated ya worse. I grew up in that town and only the sheriff and the Doc talk to me. I thought I was doing the best thing by staying away. I hoped the people in town would give ya and Samantha a chance."

Brian sniffled. "I guess you were wrong."

"I was wrong. Well, maybe I can get ya set up in the next town. I'll deal with Chigger."

"No! He's mean as a snake. I don't want ya hurt because of me." Samantha's eyes grew wide with fear.

"I don't plan on getting hurt." He looked deep into her eyes and she could feel the pull of him. He was magnetic and it became a struggle to stay away from him.

"Have ya been to the next town?" she asked, trying to change the subject from Chigger.

"Olia? I've been there. It's smaller than Winsten. They don't care about me one way or the other. The only reason I don't do business in Olia instead is the merchant at the general store won't give me a fair price for my furs. But I never had a problem."

"Smaller?" Her stomach knotted. "I was hoping to find a job and raise Brian there. But we can just go on to the next one if we need to." She mentally counted how much money she didn't have. They'd barely enough to get to Olia. She didn't have a plan, all she wanted was to keep Brian safe.

Patrick nodded. "Ya never know what the future holds." He reached out and gave her hand a gentle squeeze. "Folks might be nice."

It hurt to try to smile. Everything hurt her head, her face, her stomach, her heart. Patrick didn't want them. She'd secretly held out hope he'd come down the mountain and tell her he couldn't live without her. Her mother would have called her being fanciful. Her father would have told her it was a pipe dream and to stop wishing for what she couldn't have. She thought she'd faced reality but it hadn't hurt like now.

"Do they have a saloon there?" Brian asked.

Patrick's eyes narrowed. "Yes, why?"

"Some folks said the only job for Sam was in a saloon. Maybe they'd hire her."

Warmth flooded her face and she quickly looked away. Just one more reason for Patrick to feel sorry for her. It shamed her.

"People said that?" His voice seemed to boom throughout the cave, and she jumped.

"It was suggested a time or two," she said softly. "It's all fine. Brian and I will be just fine. If it hadn't been for the mountain lion, this trip would have gone great. We learned a lot about survival from you and we make do. Well, the beans might be a bit much but you do what you can. I'm sure we'll find a home and I'll get a job, a good job."

His eyebrow arched. "I'm not sure there will be any jobs, but we can look. It might be best if the two of ya went to town alone. Ya know what people will think if you're seen with me."

"I'm glad you were here when we needed you." She tried her hardest to smile but she didn't have one inside her. She wished she hadn't seen him again. It would just be harder when he left them again. He held a piece of her heart she knew she'd never get back. It belonged only to him. "The rain is letting up. Tomorrow should be a good travel day. How far to town do you think?"

"Not so far. You'll probably get there by nightfall tomorrow. Ya might want to camp outside of town so ya can see it in the daylight. I'm not sure you'll find a place to stay so late in the day."

Nodding her body chilled. Too bad he didn't want them. If she had to work in the saloon, it might not be so bad. "Serving drinks wouldn't be so bad. If they have a school and all I suppose we might stay." As if she had any choice.

"Is that what ya think they do? Serve drinks?"

"I did hear some singing. I can sing."

"Where exactly did ya grow up?"

"A farm in Missouri. We had a few neighbors and we went to town every Sunday for church. We didn't have a saloon. We did have a café and there were waitresses."

Patrick groaned.

"What is it?" She asked.

He glanced at Brian. "We'll talk about it later."

She nodded. Maybe he didn't approve of a nighttime job. She watched as Brian and Patrick whittled and talked. Brian had been craving attention for such a long time now. She gave him all of hers but it wasn't enough. She swallowed hard to keep the tears at bay. It wouldn't do to shroud their happiness in her despair.

"I'll heat up dinner, and then I think we all need a good night's sleep. Tomorrow will be a busy day." She opened a few cans of beans and placed them in the hot coals. "I have some tea if you like."

"Ya have tea? Mrs. Andrews didn't have any."

"I'll make you some." Avoiding his gaze was hard but it was a must. Her heart needed to be protected from more hurt.

This time Brian didn't complain as he ate. He was too busy eating and talking. She wished his happiness could be hers, but she knew the ending and Brian hadn't thought that far ahead. The pain in her heart grew as she watched them eat, and later as Patrick tucked Brian into bed. He did it with such care.

She stayed by the fire waiting to hear what he had to say about the job at the saloon. A job was a job.

Patrick gave her a slight smile as he sat on the ground next to her. He turned a bit so he was facing her. "Ya can't work in a saloon."

"Why not?"

"It's not a place for a respectable woman to work."

"I don't see how serving drinks could be so bad. I know they wear some fancy dresses and all but if the money is good…" He took her hand and rubbed the back of it with his thumb.

"Ya don't know what goes on in a place like that. Men pay for liquor and for a woman's favor."

"Favor?"

"They pay for women to entertain them in bed."

She gasped and snatched her hand back, clamping it over her mouth. Her eyes widened as she dropped her hand. "Are you telling me the truth? They are, are, whores? Oh my word." Her shoulders slumped as her last idea for survival slipped away. "When the people in town told me to work in the saloon they expected me to—?"

"Yes. I'm sorry, it's all my fault. I should have come up with some way ya could have gotten help for Brian without anyone knowing about me."

"Don't beat yourself up. We needed you and you were there for us. That's all that matters. I've missed you these past few months. There's been no one to talk to about my fears and problems. The way they shunned Brian tore my heart out. It was lonely but I do thank you for providing us with a place to live. You've done more for us than anyone else. I can never repay you for your kindness."

He leaned over and kissed her cheek, so gently, so tenderly, tears fell from her eyes. "Hey, don't cry. I thought I was doing the right thing by leaving ya alone. I figured people would forget. Ya and Brian both have such big hearts, I just thought everyone would be able to see that about ya." He leaned in again and this time his lips captured hers.

His hard masculine lips softened as he kissed her. Closing her eyes, she allowed the magic of the moment to dull her heartbreak. Kissing him was like coming home. He parted her lips with his tongue and delved it into her mouth until it found her tongue to dance with. She whimpered when he broke the kiss and he pulled her onto his lap, wrapping his arms around her, holding her tight. His strong hands stroked her back as she laid her head on his broad shoulder. He smelled of pine and smoke from the fire. She buried her face in his neck and kissed it. His body trembled. Was it from her kiss?

Lifting her face, wanting to see her eyes, he captured her lips. Her heart beat faster and faster. There wasn't anything in the whole world as good as his kiss. Just his nearness had her yearning to be closer to him. Most women she knew had called it a wifely duty. Maybe the duty part came later. He kissed her neck and behind her ear and she sighed. "I wish—"

He cut her off with another searing kiss. His tongue dueled with hers and desire flooded her. It filled her whole being. How was she going to let him go?

A rustling sound in the bushes outside of the cave alerted them and before she knew it, she'd been dumped off his lap and onto the hard dirt-packed ground.

"Go back into the back of the cave with Brian." He grabbed his gun and inched toward the entrance. He got on his belly and scanned outside. He lay very still for some time and she wondered what was going on.

By this time, Brian had wakened and his eyes were wide with fear. "It's okay. We heard an animal. I'm going to grab my rifle. Ya stay here and stay low." Brian nodded solemnly. She grabbed her rifle and shimmied on her stomach toward the entrance, trying to keep as silent as possible. The look of annoyance Patrick gave her wasn't a surprise.

"Two men. I have a feeling I know who they are. Keep your firearm near ya. I have a feeling they won't play nice."

Nodding, she felt sick. It was Stinky Sullivan and Chigger. She should have expected them, but she thought since she left in the dark of night, she wouldn't be missed so soon. Another plan gone awry. Patrick would protect them and she would help.

"Just stay low and don't move. They may become bold enough to come out in the open. I doubt they know I'm here with ya. I doubt Sheriff Todd is on their list of friends."

Her body trembled, but she got a hold of herself. No matter what, she needed to be brave for Brian. She thanked God more than once for sending Patrick to them in their time of need. She heard Ahern scream and waited for Patrick to jump up and save him. Instead, he lay still. His body tensed and he bit off a curse but he didn't flinch.

A few minutes later Stinky and Chigger walked into view. They walked cockily as though they hadn't a care in the world. Patrick cocked his gun.

"Hold it right there!"

Both men's jaws dropped as they scrambled to get to their guns. She cocked the rifle loudly and they scrambled to find cover. A shot rang out and they stopped.

"Listen, we have no beef with ya," Chigger shouted. "Just looking for some food is all. It's wet and cold out here. We just wanted a cup of coffee."

"Chigger, I know it's ya and Sullivan out there, and I know what ya plan to do. It's always best to have no witnesses when you've done the devil's work."

"Why aren't you on your damn mountain?" Stinky asked with a whine in his voice.

"I came to protect Samantha and Brian from the likes of ya."

Stinky sneered. "What's she to you? I knew it, she's used goods now. Killing her might be doing her a favor. No man will want her now. I'm surprised she isn't working at the saloon. Of course, her pay would be practically nothing.

Customers get a discount if the woman's been with an Indian. Chigger here already wired the orphanage, and they are sending someone to collect the boy."

She gasped. It didn't matter what they thought of her but Brian. How could they condemn the boy to life in the orphanage?

"Like my friend here asked. What's she to you? Are you willing to die for her? Sullivan and I are experts with guns. I'd hate for you to get hurt for nothing."

"Ya plan to kill me anyway. I'm not stupid ya know. As for Samantha and Brian, they are the closest thing I have to family and I'll gladly protect them till my last breath."

Fear, pain, and now warmth filled her. She hoped he meant it but it could be some ploy to get the men to back off.

"What about you, Samantha?" Chigger called out. "Are you willing to get the mountain man killed because of you? Why don't you come out nice and slow and the other two can go on their way?"

Before she could answer, Patrick spoke. "She stays with me as does the boy. Now, ya have to the count of three to skedaddle or I'm going to start shooting. One…"

Stinky and Chigger began to shoot. A bullet hit the ground in front of her face and she rolled out of the way. It was over before she had her gun ready to fire. Both Stinky and Chigger lay on the ground with blood on their chests.

"They're dead," she said woodenly.

"There was no choice."

"I know. Thank you for coming to our rescue, yet again. I don't know what we'll do without you."

"I want to see the dead men!" Brian ran past her and whistled. "Wow!" He turned to look at Patrick but he'd already left the cave to see to the horses.

A loud curse was heard and she grabbed Brian's hand and

climbed down to see about Ahern. As they approached, she saw blood on his coat. "Oh no! How bad is it?"

"They cut him with a knife. It's not too deep. I bet they intended to keep cutting if they thought we were holed up. Stupid fools."

Brian walked toward Patrick and stopped at his side. He took Patrick's hand. "It's my fault. Sam didn't want them to send me away."

Patrick squatted next to him. "It's not your fault at all. The fault lies with Chigger and Stinky. Their greed made them hurt many people. Good people like you and Samantha."

Her face warmed as he glanced over Brian's head at her. She felt something pass between them. For her it was love but she wasn't sure about him. He'd told her time and again they couldn't be and she had to respect his feelings.

"Do you think Chigger wired for someone to come get Brian? If so we'd best keep going to the next town."

"There's nothing in that town for ya."

"Maybe, but we won't know until we try."

"Let's go back to Wintsen," Patrick said as he lifted Brian into his arms.

"I don't see why."

"We have at least three allies there, the sheriff, the doc and the preacher."

"The preacher? He hasn't been any too nice to me or Brian," she protested.

"He's known me since I was a child and he helped me out of more than one tough spot. He'll help us."

Help them do what she didn't know.

"Let's get some sleep and head back in the morning," Patrick suggested.

"We can't just leave the bodies out here, they'll attract wild animals."

"Well darlin', just about all animals out here are wild." He grinned. "I'll pull the bodies a good ways away."

She nodded and led Brian back to the cave. "I guess we'd better get some sleep."

"Samantha? I'm afraid they'll take me away."

She pulled Brian into a hug and kissed his cheek. "No one is taking you away from me."

"Promise?"

"I promise."

THEY RODE HARD all day long with Patrick taking the lead. He kept at a good pace and planned for them to be back to town a little after nightfall. Thankfully, they had the homestead to stay in. At this point, he didn't care who knew he was staying there or not. He had plans, plans he hoped Samantha would go along with. They needed his protection and they needed a way to keep Brian safe before trouble came to find them.

Turning in the saddle, he was glad to see although weary, they were both holding up well. Their strength and resilience made him proud. He would do what needed to be done. He would protect them and hopefully it would be a good thing. Hopefully it would be the right thing for all of them.

He stopped in front of the house and jumped down off Ahern. He patted the horse's withers. Next, he lifted Brian down from in front of Samantha and finally he lifted Samantha into his arms and let her body slide against his before setting her down. Part of him hoped she felt his arousal and part of him hoped she didn't notice. He didn't want to scare her. "I'll take care of the horses, ya go on in."

"You're not taking off again?"

"No, not tonight. I am a bit hungry though." He smiled.

She laughed. "Beans coming right up."

"Please say it's a bad joke!" Brian yelled from inside.

They both laughed. Their gazes met and locked. He couldn't get enough of her beautiful blue eyes. They held love and trust and truth in them and he wanted to be worthy of it all. "I'll be back in a while." He watched her enter the house before he led both horses to the barn. They both needed a good rub down and extra feed. He wanted to check on Ahern's knife wound again. Thankfully, it wasn't in a place where the saddle rubbed it.

Once done he headed toward the house. His heart filled and beat faster knowing he had them waiting for him. He never would have thought it was something he remotely wanted but he wanted it now. The fear of rejection tore at him. He was half-Indian and she might refuse him.

He also needed to get over to the sheriff's office and report what happened with Chigger and Sullivan. There shouldn't be any question to what happened, but sometimes his word wasn't good enough. He'd eat first then see the sheriff. Always better to head off trouble if ya can. His thoughts kept drifting toward Samantha. He loved her enough to let her go but he was selfish enough to want her by his side.

When he entered the house, the smile she gave him lifted his heart. "Is dinner about ready?"

She shook her head. "I'm good but not that good. It'll be about an hour."

"I'd best take Snowstorm back to the livery and stop by to tell the sheriff what happened."

"We'll be here when you get back." She turned toward the stove and gave whatever she was cooking, a stir.

"Hurry back!" Brian told him.

"I'll do my best." He put his cap on and headed outside. He coaxed Snowstorm into his bridle and walked him into town. Most places were already closed for the day. He passed the saloon and heard the music and clinking of glasses. Samantha really was green if she didn't know what went on in there. The lights at the livery were on and he walked into the barn with Snowstorm.

"Returning the horse you stole?" A big burly man with blond hair asked him, none too politely.

"This here is Snowstorm he belongs to the sheriff. Which stall should I put him in?"

"I know what horse it is. I figure you took him without permission. That's horse stealin' and that's a hanging offense." The man smiled, looking pleased with himself.

"I guess that would be for the sheriff to decide." He led Snowstorm to an empty stall, put him in, and closed the stall door.

"Maybe I should get the sheriff." The man crossed his big arms across his chest.

"I'm heading to his office now. Sheriff Todd and I go way back." He turned and left, listening to the man sputter. People were all the same. It was only one block to the sheriff's office, and he made fast work of getting there. He opened the door and nodded.

"Find them? Were they okay? Chigger and Sullivan left town right after you did." He wiped his chin with a napkin from the tray of food on his desk.

"Samantha and Brian are fine. Chigger and Sullivan are dead. They ambushed us and came up the losers. I left their bodies out there."

"I don't suppose anyone would pay to bury them here. Did you find out why they were after Samantha?"

"She was the only one alive who could point a finger at them. They led that wagon train to its death and stole all the money. Sullivan took off with all the money and Chigger just caught up with him recently. Chigger threatened Samantha."

"So that's why she left? Makes sense. Are you hungry? Anita at the diner always brings me more than I can eat."

"Samantha is cooking us dinner. Did ya know she was thinking about working in the saloon? She thought she'd just be a waitress." Patrick smiled. "She's as innocent as they come."

"I'm afraid she's in for a big upset. A man from the orphanage is planning to be here in two days to take Brian back. I just got the telegram. I know she loves that boy."

He sighed and nodded. "Yes she does."

"You know, I doubt the man would climb up into the mountains for one small boy. You might want to consider taking them back up there with you."

"Wish I could but it would only ruin their lives. People have shunned them because of me."

"Well it wasn't just because of you. Unbelievably, they are more in a snit that she lived with you. Rumor has it you're a very virile man." He laughed. "Damned if you don't. Damned if you do."

Patrick nodded as he turned the doorknob. "I'm damned all right."

"See you around."

"Thanks for the use of the horse."

"Anytime. Now go and eat a home cooked meal."

Patrick opened the door and strode outside. He walked up the boardwalk, his heels making clicking noises with each step. The sound of spurs against the wood always made him cringe. Soon he was out of town and the soft glow of the oil lamp beckoned from the homestead. His heart was in his throat. He knew what he had to do, he just didn't know if she'd go along.

He opened the door and there they were both laughing. It was good to see them happy.

"Oh good, you're just in time. Why don't you and Brian wash up and we can eat."

He nodded and joined Brian at the basin filled with water. He wasn't much for washing up before meals but if it made her happy, he'd do it.

"How's the sheriff?" she asked.

"Good. He was glad to be rid of Sullivan and Chigger. He did have some bad news though." He paused and glanced at Brian. "A man is coming to collect Brian."

Samantha gasped and put her hands over her mouth. Tears filled her eyes as she shook her head. "They can't have him! Oh, we should have gone on to the next town."

"They're going to take me away? They'll beat me for sure." Brian swallowed hard and tried to appear brave. "It'll be fine, Sam. I lived that way for a long time and I can do it again." His shoulders slouched and his smile wobbled.

"I have a solution if you're willing. I don't want an answer right away. I want ya to think it through tonight. There are two options. I take Brian to live with me. The other option is Sam marries me and we both take ya up the mountain. Either way ya are not going back to that place." Samantha started to open her mouth and he put his hand up. "No answers today. Ya need to think about it. If I take him, you'll get to see him and ya can live here in the homestead. No worries, I'll provide for ya."

Samantha nodded and quickly glanced away. If only he could see her eyes. He had no idea what she thought.

"Thanks Patrick! I didn't want to go back, not ever!" Brian climbed off his chair and hugged Patrick. "I'm glad you found me that day in the barn."

He rubbed the top of Brian's head until the boy's hair stood up on end. "I'm glad too. I'm glad I found ya both." He stared at Samantha but she didn't look up at him. His heart pinged and his chest squeezed. He was the one who didn't want an answer right away but he wished he knew what she was thinking.

"I have dishes to wash." She stood and began to clear the table, avoiding his gaze at all costs. Brian sat in a chair close to the fire and grabbed his knife and a stick.

Patrick stood next to Samantha. "We'll talk after Brian is in bed. There are a lot of considerations and I want ya to make an informed decision." He took her hand and gave it a gentle squeeze. "It'll all work out, you'll see." He turned and walked toward Brian, wondering if she would decide to stay in town.

Her hands shook so hard she was sure she'd drop the dishes. There were two choices, one with her and one without her. If he'd really wanted her to come, he wouldn't have offered her the chance to stay at the homestead. She couldn't take advantage of his generosity any longer. He was a loner who enjoyed his solitude. Taking Brian on would be more than enough for a man who didn't want others around. She really had only one choice and it would break her heart to see them go. They'd have to leave tomorrow or the day after. Who knew when the orphanage man would be here? Her heart ached and she had a feeling the ache would never leave. Brian's safety was most important. What she wanted or needed didn't matter. She would keep busy with something. She had thought a vegetable garden would be a good thing to have.

Drying her hands, she watched Patrick and Brian whittling together. Brian would be safe. It would be hard to say good-bye but there really wasn't anything she could do about it. He'd be happy living with Patrick and she'd have to be content.

"Brian, it's getting late. It's time for bed."

"Have you decided?" Brian asked eagerly.

"Brian, we'll all decide tomorrow." Patrick told him.

Brian nodded and went into the bedroom.

"Patrick, I'm really tired too."

He grabbed her hand and pulled her toward him until she stood toe to toe with him. "Please, can we talk?" He stared into her eyes and she couldn't read him.

"Sure, of course." She stepped away and walked to one of the chairs in front of the fireplace.

Patrick grabbed a blanket and arranged it on the floor. "Come sit with me."

Nodding, she did as he bade. It was as if she had no will of her own. Kneeling, she eventually made herself comfortable on the floor. What was expected of her? Did he mean to let her down easily?

"You're upset."

"No, yes. Yes, I am upset. I'm upset that someone is coming to take Brian away. I love that child with my whole heart. I had hoped I could keep him."

"Ya still could. The choice is yours." He cocked his left brow waiting for an answer.

"Ever since you rescued me, I've brought you nothing but trouble. I've invaded your serene life and made things difficult for you. I know a man like you treasures his freedom and I'll not tie you down. It would be best if you took Brian. I trust you and I know he'll be safe with you. He loves you."

"And ya?"

"I love him and I know he loves me. I feel like a mother to him. A mother would do what's best for her child. You can teach him to trap. You are a man of integrity and I would like him to learn how to grow into a man from you."

Patrick took her hand into his warm one. He stroked the back of her hand with his thumb. He reached over with his other hand and placed a strand of her hair behind her ear. "Ya are so beautiful. Your skin is so soft, your hair is glorious and your eyes glow. Sometimes I think they glow just for me, and other times I know they do not. I wish I could be the one to make ya happy. I wish your heart felt as mine does. I understand I wouldn't want to be shunned by the town if I were ya. Ya did nothing wrong, and they turned their backs on ya. Ya deserve a husband who can hold his head high."

"The heck with other people, and don't you dare think you can't hold your head high. You are the best man I have ever met. There hasn't been a day I didn't think of you, long for you. I know you don't want me with you, and I can accept your decision. I just didn't know being apart would hurt so much. Brian comes first, and you can keep him safe."

"I'd like to keep ya safe too. I lay in bed at night wondering what your day was like. I too have longings and I miss ya like crazy."

"What are you saying, exactly?"

He kissed the palm of her hand. "I love ya, Samantha, and I want ya to be my wife. Will ya marry me?"

Her jaw dropped. "You really love me? You left us here. How could you love me yet leave me?"

"I left ya because I love ya. I thought maybe it would be better for ya to be with yar own kind. I have a past with the people of this town and they can't get past my heritage. I didn't want ya painted with the same brush. I wanted better for ya and for Brian. But now I'm being selfish and trying to do what is in my heart. I want to have choices and I choose ya."

Closing her eyes, she tried to think. He sounded so sincere and the look in his eyes was one of love. She wouldn't miss the town or its people as long as she had Brian and Patrick. Her stomach fluttered. There really wasn't much to think about after all. Opening her eyes, she smiled. This time she leaned over and kissed him. His facial hair tickled her and she smiled against his lips. Joy filled her as he smiled against her lips too.

"Is that your answer?"

Pulling away, she put a finger over his mouth. "No decisions until tomorrow."

He growled and pinned her to the floor. "I can't get enough of ya. I could spend the rest of my life staring at your beautiful face."

"I'm not pretty. I don't know why you think I am."

"Just because your parents didn't tell ya don't mean it's not true. Ya have a beautiful soul, heart, and face. I want to be with ya as man and wife. I want to lay skin to skin with ya."

"Patrick, I've never, and my mother never told me anything. I don't know how. Maybe I'd make a bad wife."

"Shh. Your response to my kisses makes me believe ya will be a very good wife. I think we can have a happy life. We have Brian and soon children…" he sat up and put a lot of distance between them. "Damn, what the hell am I thinking? I'm sorry I built up your hopes with my foolish dreams. I can't, I won't bring a child of mine into the world to be treated like a dog. Ya make me forget myself. I suppose it's best if I take Brian and ya stay here."

A coldness swept through her and from his expression there was no changing his mind. Her hopes shriveled, as did her happiness. "I understand." She stood up and went into the bedroom without looking at him. Numbly she changed into her nightdress and brushed her hair before she braided it. Tomorrow, it would be best if they left tomorrow. Her chest burned, as did the back of her eyes, but she refused to cry. It was hard on Patrick too.

Sleep evaded her and as soon as the rooster crowed, she was already dressed and ready for the day. She made tea, eggs, bacon, and biscuits with jam. She'd give them the extra biscuits to take. She choked back a sob. To take with them. She heard them get up and soon they were at the table ready to eat.

"This will be our last meal for a while so, Brian, I made your favorites. I'm so excited for you and your new life. I know Patrick will take very good care of you." She drank some tea to alleviate her dry throat. Her words sounded forced.

"Patrick explained things to me, Sam. We'll get to see you all the time. Well, maybe not much in the winter but the rest of the year we can visit." He bravely held back his tears. "I have my things all ready to go. Ahern will stay with you."

Patrick nodded. No one ate much and the rest of the meal was spent in silence. "We'd best get ready."

Brian got up and went to his room.

"I packed some food for you. Do you need anything else?" She foolishly hoped he'd say yes, he needed her. She waited but no such declaration was made. At least Brian would be safe.

"Thanks, the food is more than enough. I'll try to get down here once a month if possible. I'm sorrier than ya will ever know."

"Maybe we could get married and not, well you know."

"Not possible. I want ya with everything in me. I wouldn't be able to keep from touching ya."

"I see. I'll walk you out."

Brian ran ahead of them carrying a bedroll and a canteen. She started to follow when Patrick grabbed her hand, stopping her. He stroked her bottom lip with the pad of his thumb. "I never meant to hurt ya."

"I know." The heaviness of her heart became unbearable. "I need you to leave while I keep my tears at bay for Brian's sake."

Patrick let her go and followed her outside. She hugged

and kissed Brian and exchanged a long look with Patrick. She stood in the middle of the road until she could see them no more. Tears streamed down her face and she ran into the house. Heartbroken, she went to her room and lay across the bed and sobbed, big gut wrenching sobs. She didn't stop until there were no more tears. Her eyes swelled and hurt and her ribs ached from sobbing. For a moment she had it all and now she had nothing.

CHAPTER TEN

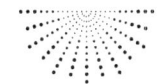

Eight weeks later

She bent over the big hot tub of water, stirring the clothes she'd just scrubbed against the scrub board. Luckily, the town took pity on her and allowed her to do their laundry. That's how they acted too, as if they were doing her a big favor. Next, she checked the clothes in the cold-water tub and one by one, she wrung the water from the garments before she put them through the wringer. After that, she put them on the line to dry and then she'd iron them. It was backbreaking work, but it was honest work. Most days she worked from sun up into the late hours of the evening.

There was no way she'd let herself get behind. They were probably looking for a reason to fire her. It kept her busy and she didn't have much time to dwell. She hadn't heard from Patrick or Brian in about eight weeks. Eight excruciating, long weeks. Her heart was in her throat half the time and she had no appetite. Her clothes hung on her, but she didn't care. She didn't care about the haughty looks she got from the women or the leering ones from the men. She didn't care about her appearance and she didn't care about anything happening in the town.

All she did was wake up and spend her days doing laundry. Her hands were so red from the scrub board and the lye soap she didn't even recognize them as her own. Her back ached constantly and she had burn marks on her hands and arms from the iron. She often looked down the trail that led to the mountain for her two guys but no one was ever there. Each long day chipped away a piece of her heart until it finally lay shattered and she hadn't a clue how to put it back together.

They'd forgotten her, plain and simple. She reminded herself every day how lucky she was to have a roof over her head. The vegetable garden she planned never happened. She just didn't have the time or energy to put one in. She carefully saved each penny so she could leave and start again, someday. It would do her good to be away from the mountain trail. It hurt too much to keep staring and waiting.

Maybe she'd never leave. There was always the hope Brian would return. At least he was in good hands, but it didn't console her battered heart. The man from the orphanage had arrived just as expected but Sheriff Todd sent him on his way, telling him he'd never seen Brian. It was a big relief. One less thing to worry about. There were times she wondered if she'd made it all up, the love given and received by both Brian and Patrick. Surely, they'd have come down the mountain. Maybe one of them was hurt. They didn't have Ahern to ride to get help.

Wiping the sweat from her brow, she bent backward to stretch her aching back. She had no rights to Brian. She'd always wanted a family of her own but now it didn't appeal to her. She already had a family and her imagination didn't stretch far enough to think of another man. Blaming Patrick did no good. He made his decision from experience. Why did people have to be so judgmental? Why couldn't they all get along? They attend church services every Sunday without fail but the rest of the week, their actions were not ones of a Christian.

Even the poorest of poor avoided her. It ate at her soul. Memories were a sad comfort at night. The house was so quiet she was thinking of getting a dog. Ahern listened but he was Patrick's horse. She'd tried to get someone to take the horse back up the mountain but no one offered. Perhaps she should return the horse herself. She sighed. It would probably bring nothing but more heartbreak. She couldn't handle more, not right now.

"This is unacceptable!" Noreen Black screeched as she threw one of her husband's shirts at Samantha's face. Her black hair was pulled back so tight it made her eyes look like they were popping out. "There is a big tear in the back and the front of it is scorched. I need to buy a brand new shirt."

Samantha picked up the shirt and knew she wasn't the one who ruined it. In fact, Noreen refused to bring her laundry. More than likely, she did it herself.

"You'll have to pay for it, you know. I highly doubt you've made enough to cover the cost. This is a fine shirt."

"I haven't washed a shirt so fine. I'm afraid you're mistaken, Mrs. Black. You refused to do business with me, or have you forgotten the scene you made at the general store?"

"How dare you talk to me that way? Maybe you need to go up that mountain where you belong. You sure as hell don't belong here. I'll send the sheriff by to collect the three dollars from you." She turned and stalked off.

Crestfallen, Samantha had had enough. More than enough for one lifetime. Even with all her hard work, she didn't have three dollars. No one would take her word over Noreen's. Her husband owned the bank. She kicked the ground in frustration. She'd finally been pushed too hard.

She left all the laundry right where it was and hurried to the house. There was only so much a person could take. She'd return Ahern and then go down the other side of the mountain. Anywhere but here would be good. Packing her few belongings didn't take long. She smiled as she put cans of beans in a sack along with shotgun shells and flint. The days were getting longer and there was plenty of daylight left.

The expected sadness of leaving her home didn't happen. She saddled Ahern and they rode in the direction of the mountain. There was no sense staying to listen to the sheriff. He might be a friend but what Noreen wanted, she got.

The weather was perfect all day and she found the cave they had stayed in before. Everything would be fine.

"But you promised," Brian pleaded as he stared at Patrick. They both sat on the stairs, taking a break. "You keep saying we'll go but we never do." He crossed his arms in front of him and gave a sullen look.

"I know and I'm sorry."

"Is it because you love her? I could help you out with what to say."

Patrick's lips twitched. "Oh really? Like what?"

"Women like to hear they are the most beautiful person in the whole wide world. They want to know your heart goes pitter pat when you see them. What does pitter pat mean?"

Patrick nodded. Brian was so serious in his advice. "It means your heart beats faster."

"Oh. And a way to a man's heart is through their stomach. That means you have to like her cookin' even if it's beans."

He leaned closer to Patrick, his eyes wide, and stared. "Do you need me to explain it again?"

"I think I've got it. It's more complicated than that, Brian."

Brian leaned back. "It's about children. I know your children would be nice and all but, I'm still going to be the oldest. The oldest is the smartest and bravest. Women always go on and on about babies." He rolled his eyes.

"Where'd ya here that, the part about the babies?"

"Solomon. He said he left more than a few women with babies. Every woman wants one but when they find out they are having one they act all crazy and he knew it was time to leave. Is that why we left? Is Sam having a baby? I didn't see her acting crazy like except for when she said I couldn't have coffee. Maybe Sam is the type that doesn't go crazy. Don't you want to see your child?"

He sighed and ran his fingers through his hair. "No, son, Samantha isn't having a baby and I certainly wouldn't leave one of my children behind."

"Well let's go. There is no reason for us not to go and ya did promise." Brian widened his eyes while waiting for an answer.

"I suppose you're right."

"Yay! I'll get packed." He stood and ran into the house.

He was plumb out of excuses. It'd been one of the hardest thing's he'd ever done, saying goodbye to Samantha. His reasons were valid but up here in the mountains, they didn't seem to matter anymore. Thank God, he had Brian to keep him company or he'd have gone crazy. Even with Brian, a big part of him didn't feel whole. Samantha owned the biggest part of his heart.

Brian stuck his head out the door. "You coming or what?"

The boy was persistent. Patrick stood and went into the house. "No complaining about eating beans."

"Okay, just hurry!"

It didn't take long to gather the things they would need. They could only take as much as they could carry. He missed his damn horse too. "Let's go."

The weather was nice and they made good time. Brian was curious about every animal they saw. He knew their names but not how or where they lived. It made the time go by faster as he explained things to him. There was a part of him anxious to see her and a part of him dreading it. He didn't even have a valid excuse as to why they hadn't been down for a visit and he realized just how wrong he was to keep Brian from her. He hadn't thought about it that way before, but now he felt ashamed. He strived to be better than that, or so he'd thought. He wasn't sure about anything anymore.

They made camp for the night and ate the dreaded beans. Brian didn't complain once.

"Do you think she misses me?" Brian sounded anxious.

"With her whole heart, I imagine. She'll be overjoyed to see ya."

Brian yawned and lay on his bedroll. "You too." He closed his eyes.

He doubted it. He'd practically insisted they get married then refused to marry her. He probably wasn't one of her favorites. He'd be lucky if she gave him a hello. He was leaving it all up to God. Some things were meant to be and others not. He was at a loss.

He lay down and closed his eyes. All he could see was Samantha, her smile, her hair, her lips. What a fool he'd been. Part of the reason the town didn't accept him was because his father was the town drunk. He'd be a better parent, he hoped. Finally, he slept.

SAMANTHA SAW a glimpse of two people and she quickly got off the trail. She didn't want or need any trouble and predators were everywhere. Sliding off Ahern, she took the reins and guided the horse behind a group of boulders. Her heart beat out of her chest as she waited for them to pass. They were so close, she held her breath but Ahern whinnied rather loudly. Still she shrank back against the rocks, hoping. She didn't hear anything and she grabbed the rifle when Ahern broke loose and headed for the trail. *Lord have mercy*. She was done for. Scrambling, she flung herself behind a different set of rocks and waited. Her heart beat faster and faster until she heard Brian's voice call out for her. Did they have Brian too?

"Samantha, it's me Patrick. Can ya answer me?"

She swallowed hard.

"Do you think she's hurt?" She didn't like the panic in Brian's voice.

"I'm here, "she called as she stepped out into the open. A better sight she'd never seen, Patrick and Brian safe and sound. She took a few steps toward them and the next thing she knew, she was in Patrick's arms. He swung her around before he soundly kissed her.

"I want to hug her too!"

Patrick let her go and she dropped to her knees, taking Brian into her arms. She hugged him to her tightly and began to cry.

"Tell her she's the most beautiful woman in the whole world," he told Patrick.

He helped her to her feet and dried her tears. "He's right ya know. Ya are the most beautiful woman in the whole world."

"Tell her you'll eat her beans," Brian urged.

"I'll eat your beans." His expression was so earnest she laughed.

"What's going on here?" She gazed at Brian then Patrick. "Is this some type of joke?"

Patrick removed his hat and hit his thigh with it. "I'm no good at this. We were coming down to see ya."

Her smile faded. "It's about time. I waited every day for over two months. I even had a job."

Patrick grabbed her hand. "Why are yar hands so red and rough?"

Quickly she snatched them back. "I took in wash. Until recently, when Noreen claimed I tore her husband's shirt and scorched it. I never washed any of their clothes. She expected me to pay three dollars for the darn thing so I left. I'm up here to return Ahern to you and visit for a day or two then I'm off."

"Off to where?"

"Why do you care?" She folded her arms across her front and frowned.

Patrick's eyes grew wide. "Why do I care? Woman, I told ya how beautiful ya are and I promised to eat your beans. Damn it! I should have used my own words but Brian, well never mind. Samantha, my love for ya runs deep in my heart. When we're apart all I do is think about ya. I miss ya, I worry about ya, and I love ya. Ya bring the sunshine into my life and I feel as though I'd wilt without ya."

"Patrick, I love you too but—"

He took a step forward and placed his finger over her lips. "No buts. We get married and do it all proper. If ya want to move back to town, we can do it. I just want ya happy."

She nodded and he pulled her into his strong arms. Wrapping her arms around his waist, tears sprung. She was home, right here in his arms. She smiled at Brian who looked on. "I want to be up here on your mountain."

Patrick took a step back and cradled her cheek in his palm. "Are ya sure?"

"Yes."

"Then let's get going, we're halfway to town and we can get married."

"I don't know about going back there. I don't have three dollars for Noreen's lie."

"Don't ya worry about that." He smiled. "No more worries."

EPILOGUE

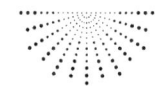

Patrick held Samantha's hand, rubbing his thumb along the back of it. "Finally finished. Now one more to go."

She glanced around, making sure they were alone. "Maybe I won't have to be so quiet at night. Ya did a beautiful job on our bedroom. Thank you, Patrick."

"Ya might actually take off all your clothes at one time."

She swatted his shoulder. "What if Brian needed me in the middle of the night? But I have a feeling we'll have a lot of fun. I'm so glad you changed your mind about children."

Patrick placed his hand on her growing belly. "Me too. Now that we're married the town's people aren't as rude."

"They are only slightly rude." She laughed. "When's bedtime?"

He pulled her to him and kissed her until she squirmed in need. "In about five hours, I'd say."

His arousal was easily felt as he held her. "Feels like you'll be suffering."

He cocked his left brow. "There's always the barn. I know how much ya like the hay."

"Don't even joke about that, Patrick. Hay is scratchy. You could have at least warned me it wouldn't be a good idea." She laughed, stood on tiptoe and gave her husband a passion filled kiss. "I'm so glad I have you."

"Me too."

"Oh yuck! Why can't you be like other married folks? You know, the ones who fight then don't talk to each other?" He shook his head at them. "The room is done! Does that mean you'll start work on mine soon?"

"Yes—" Patrick started.

"Great! See ya!" He ran back outside.

Samantha chuckled. "Have I told you how much I love you today?"

"No. Not a word but we can go into the bedroom and ya can show me."

"Set the bed up and maybe we'll have some fun in five hours."

THE END

I'm so pleased you chose to read Love So Deep, and it's my sincere hope that you enjoyed the story. I would appreciate if you'd consider posting a review. This can help an author tremendously in obtaining a readership. My many thanks. ~ Kathleen

ABOUT THE AUTHOR

Sexy Cowboys and the Women Who Love Them...
Finalist in the 2012 and 2015 RONE Awards.
Top Pick, Five Star Series from the Romance Review.
Kathleen Ball writes contemporary and historical western romance with great emotion and
memorable characters. Her books are award winners and have appeared on best sellers lists including: Amazon's Best Seller's List, All Romance Ebooks, Bookstrand, Desert Breeze Publishing and Secret Cravings Publishing Best Sellers list. She is the recipient of eight Editor's Choice Awards, and The Readers' Choice Award for Ryelee's Cowboy.
Winner of the Lear diamond award Best Historical Novel- Cinders' Bride
There's something about a cowboy

- facebook.com/kathleenballwesternromance
- x.com/kballauthor
- instagram.com/author_kathleenball

OTHER BOOKS BY KATHLEEN

Lasso Spring Series
Callie's Heart
Lone Star Joy
Stetson's Storm

Dawson Ranch Series
Texas Haven
Ryelee's Cowboy

Cowboy Season Series
Summer's Desire
Autumn's Hope
Winter's Embrace
Spring's Delight

Mail Order Brides of Texas
Cinder's Bride
Keegan's Bride
Shane's Bride
Tramp's Bride
Poor Boy's Christmas

Oregon Trail Dreamin'
We've Only Just Begun
A Lifetime to Share
A Love Worth Searching For
So Many Roads to Choose

The Settlers

Greg
Juan
Scarlett

Mail Order Brides of Spring Water Books 1-3

Tattered Hearts
Shattered Trust
Glory's Groom

Mail Order Brides of Spring Water Books 4-6

Battered Souls
Faltered Beginnings
Fairer Than Any

Romance on the Oregon Trail Books 1-3

Cora's Courage
Luella's Longing
Dawn's Destiny

Romance on the Oregon Trail Books 4-5

Terra's Trial
Candle Glow and Mistletoe

The Kavanagh Brothers Books 1-3

Teagan: Cowboy Strong
Quinn: Cowboy Risk
Brogan: Cowboy Pride

The Kavanagh Brothers Books 4-6

Sullivan: Cowboy Protector
Donnell: Cowboy Scrutiny

Murphy: Cowboy Deceived

The Kavanagh Brothers Books 7-10
Fitzpatrick: Cowboy Reluctant
Angus: Cowboy Bewildered
Rafferty: Cowboy Trail Boss
Shea: Cowboy Chance

Mail Order Brides of Pine Crossing
Alanna
Briana

The Greatest Gift
Love So Deep
Luke's Fate
Whispered Love
Love Before Midnight
I'm Forever Yours
Finn's Fortune
Glory's Groom

Printed in Great Britain
by Amazon